THE
MIDNIGHT
WAR
OF
MATEO
MARTINEZ

THE
MIDNIGHT
WAR
OF
MATEO
MARTINEZ

-ROBIN YARDI-

 CAROLRHODA BOOKS
MINNEAPOLIS

Carolrhoda Books
A division of Lerner Publishing Group, Inc.
241 First Avenue North
Minneapolis, MN 55401 USA

For reading levels and more information, look up this title at www.lernerbooks.com.

Paper: © Oleg Golovnev/Shutterstock.com

Main body text set in Bembo Std regular 12.5/17.
Typeface provided by Monotype Typography.

Library of Congress Cataloging-in-Publication Data

Yardi, Robin.
    The midnight war of Mateo Martinez / by Robin Yardi.
        p. cm.
    Summary: "Mateo, a Mexican-American fourth grader from California, spots two skunks stealing his sister's trike. He launches a crusade to retrieve the trike and soon learns that the skunks are not only thieves—they can talk, too!"
    — Provided by publisher.
        ISBN 978-1-4677-8306-4 (lb : alk. paper)
        ISBN 978-1-4677-9561-6 (eb pdf : alk. paper)
        [1. Skunks—Fiction. 2. War—Fiction. 3. Mexican Americans—Fiction.]
    I. Title.
    PZ7.1.Y37Mi 2016
    [Fic]—dc23   2015016191

Manufactured in the United States of America
1 – SB – 12/31/15

For you, when you're trying to understand things and you're not getting it right . . . yet

1.
The Crime

Nobody believed me when I said two skunks stole my old trike.

But I'd seen those stinkers take it.

Swear.

The night of the stolen trike, my mom made me come home after I had dinner with my best friend, Ashwin, 'cause we had school the next day. Ashwin always dares me to see who can drink the most of his mom's chai, and I always win, so I was on my way back from the bathroom in the middle of the night. Waking up to pee three times is a small price to pay for victory. That's what I think, anyway, even if my mom doesn't agree.

I checked the window, and everything seemed okay at first. I snuck a peek at my brand new silver-and-blue bike. Mom and Dad gave it to me in October, when I turned nine. I call it Steed. You know, like a knight's shining steed.

Our house is on this tiny one-block street in Santa

Barbara: Caballero Road. *Caballero* actually means "knight" in Spanish. I don't speak Spanish, but my dad does. Well, to me, that street name has always been a sign that I was supposed to be a knight. Like, for real. If your home is a castle, and my house totally is, then the driveway is a drawbridge. The sidewalk's a moat. My bedroom's even like a watchtower—I have a window right over the driveway, with a view straight out to Caballero Road. It's my job to keep a lookout, and that's what I was doing the first time I saw the skunks.

Seeing Steed out there made me smile even though I was sleepy, but then I heard this weird creak and leaned a little closer to my window. I squinted up and down the driveway, checking everything out. Something was missing from the dark jumble of stuff by the garage, and I was pretty sure what it was. My rusty old trike doesn't shine in the dark anymore, like Steed does, but the right back-wheel has this creak, and I definitely heard that. I don't ride the trike or anything, but my little sister, Mila, does. And I always have to make sure she puts the trike back where it's supposed to be. That night, the trike should have been where *I* used to park it when I was a little kid. It shouldn't have been out on the corner or sideways in the dirt, and it definitely shouldn't have been rolling down the driveway.

But it was.

My breath was making the glass all foggy. I rubbed it away so I could see better, and at first I thought the trike was rolling by itself. I don't know, like being pushed by the wind. But when the driveway light clicked on, I saw them. Two little black-and-white skunks, one on each pedal, holding onto the handlebars, with their tails high in the air. One skunk went up, the other went down.

Up-down, up-down, up-down, right out onto the sidewalk. When they got to the street, the skunk on the right pulled hard on the handlebar, and they wobbled around the corner.

"That's weird," I said, leaning so close my nose touched the glass.

I waited for a few minutes, but nothing else happened. Staring into the dark to see if the skunks would come back, my head felt all fuzzy. My eyes went all blinky. I flopped onto my bed, kicking at the covers, thinking, *Two skunks can't steal a trike. No way.*

I kept popping up onto my elbows to peek out the window, but pretty soon my head was too sleep-fogged to even look. I jerked awake a couple times and wiped some drool off my cheek. But I never heard that rusty creak again.

Did I fail in my solemn duty as a watchman—as a knight? What was I supposed to do, raise an alarm? Even half asleep, I guess I knew nobody would believe me. I knew what Mom and Dad would say.

And after a while, even I thought those skunks had to be a dream.

But they weren't.

2.
The Smile

The next morning, I was crunching a huge bite of cereal when I remembered my dream that wasn't really a dream. It squirted back into my brain.

"Last night, two skunks *stole* my old trike," I said. Little bits of cereal exploded out of my mouth and oozed down my chin.

My little sister, Mila, laughed.

I kicked her under the table.

Not hard.

But, you know, just to keep her in line.

"That's a funny dream, Mateo," Mom said, putting the milk away. Then she smiled at me over the rim of her coffee cup. Whenever she smiled that smile, I smiled back. I was always dreaming up strange stuff, and I loved making Mom laugh at breakfast, before it was time for all of us to leave the house.

So I forgot all about the skunks and that old trike.

I forgot about protecting my castle and being a knight.

But only for a while.

Mom stacked our cereal bowls in a heap and sploshed them into the kitchen sink. "Time to go," she said, clicking across the kitchen. Her smile was gone. "And, Mateo, no more leaving Mila behind. You have to wait for her and cross Las Positas *together*."

"I will," I said, barely moving my mouth.

Mila laughed again, but I didn't kick her.

It's not *me* that leaves *Mila* behind, but I could tell Mom wasn't in the mood to hear that excuse again. Besides, a knight does his duty without complaint. Mostly.

Mom stopped at the door to the garage and scooped her keys out of the bowl. "I mean it, Mateo. If you still want to walk to school with Ashwin, then you have to be responsible for Mila. Otherwise I'll just drive you both."

"I said I'll do it!" I told her. Mom gave me a different kind of look, the one I hated, the one that said, *Please don't make me late for work.* She scooped up her purse, a stack of papers, and her black laptop. She stopped for a second in the doorway to the garage, holding the door open with her shoulder. "And hold her hand at the light, mijo. It's your job to keep her safe."

Mom didn't wait for me to answer. The door to the garage slammed shut behind her.

Bang.

So I zipped my lunch into my backpack and pushed Mila out the front door. I wanted to get to the side-walk before Mom got her car out of the garage, so she would *see* me taking Mila. I thumped down the steps, with Mila ahead of me. The garage door groaned open, and the brakes on Mom's old car squealed. I walked fast down the driveway while Mila shuffled up to me every few steps, her backpack drumming on her butt.

We went past the shed and all our dusty old junk.

Past the tangle of hoses and extension cords my dad always forgets to put away.

And past the place where I should have checked for the old trike.

At the sidewalk, Mila stopped to wave to Mom.

"Bye, Mommy," Mila shouted, hopping up and down.

I didn't wave, but I watched until Mom's car turned the corner. Mom didn't wave back at Mila. She was holding a coffee cup in her hand. I don't think she even saw me. I started walking again, just a little too fast. Mila's black cowgirl boots went *bam-bam-bam*, and I knew she was following me, so I just kept going without looking back.

Mila caught up right before the corner, and I grabbed the straps on my backpack so she couldn't hold my hand, 'cause we weren't even close to Las Positas. That's the only time I would ever be caught holding hands with my little sister. But she didn't stop and try to grab my hand or even slow down.

Bam! Bam! Bam! She zoomed around the corner with her backpack shaking. So I didn't have time to think about the trike or the skunks or anything.

"Mila," I growled. "Wait up!"

I started to run.

The day before, someone—I don't even know who—had seen Mila crossing Las Positas by herself, not holding anybody's hand, and called my mom. Las Positas is a super busy street, so I almost got in huge trouble. What I guess that someone didn't notice was me and Ashwin running right behind Mila, shouting at her to wait up. Mila thinks she's all big now because she's going to real school. But she isn't actually in real school. She's only in TK, transitional kindergarten. If you had asked me, I would have said she was too little for that too—she just turned five last month—but Mom did not ask me. If it's my job to hold Mila's hand when we are crossing Las Positas, then I think it should be Mila's job to *wait up*.

I ran a little faster.

I was almost to the end of the block.

When I turned the corner, I saw Mila using the crosswalk by herself, and I kinda tripped a little, but she had only gotten to Castillo Street, and she's allowed to do that one on her own as long as I'm watching. Well, I *was* watching, just from pretty far away. I caught my balance, grabbed my backpack straps, and pounded my feet on the sidewalk. I couldn't risk having Mila get to Las Positas without me again. No way was I going to let Mom drive me to school like a kindergartener.

I put my head down and tried to ignore the cramp in my side.

Mila moved pretty fast for a little kid when she wanted to.

Actually, she moved pretty fast *period*.

I found her standing on top of one of those big rocks across from Oak Park, rocking back and forth on her heels. I bent over my knees, panting. "I said wait up, Mila—you're gonna get me in trouble! And we're supposed to wait for Ashwin too. That's the whole point of taking you."

She made this little scrunched-up face, didn't answer, and then—*bam!*—she jumped down next to me and started walking again. I didn't really have a choice. I had to go with her. Ashwin would just have to catch up with us. I stuck next to her, but I still didn't hold her hand.

That's when I thought about it again.

The trike, I mean—not her hand.

That old trike!

Had it been there in the driveway when we left home?

I couldn't remember, and that felt wrong.

Before the night of the stolen trike, I thought I basically knew what was going on in all the backyards and garages in our neighborhood, even the ones I was never allowed to go in. Like, I knew that Mr. Mendoza had twelve fruit trees but he never picked any fruit. His backyard could have been a medieval battlefield, slippery with the blood of slain plums. Sometimes I wondered what happened in all those backyards and garages when I had to go to school and wasn't around to keep an eye on things. I never knew I had to worry about what was going on at night too, and I definitely never knew I had to worry about *skunks*.

Dad doesn't really get my obsession with knighthood, or with books, but he always smiles when I tell him I've been watching over the neighborhood. His truck has a magnetic sign on the door that says *Xavier's Electric*, with a thunderbolt on the bottom. I used to think he was like a secret superhero. This was before I knew about knights. Now I know he's just a fancy contractor. I don't mean "just" like it's not something important. He pays his workers good and he has tons of awesome tools, but now I know he can't, like, fly.

Dad does have the heart of a superhero, though. He says you have to keep an eye on your street, do your duty, and take pride in your work. So when I remembered the skunks again, I felt like I let him down. If I was right about what I saw, then two skunks were out in the neighborhood somewhere on an old red trike, and nobody knew but me.

But I didn't know what to *do* about what I maybe knew.

I thought, again, for the tiniest second, about telling Mila about the skunks, to see what she would say. But she was only five, and I didn't think she knew *anything*. She was marching along the sidewalk with her hands on her straps. She was getting pretty far ahead again too. Her hunched-up shoulders, jiggling backpack, and smacking-the-sidewalk boots all said, "I'm big enough! I'm big enough! I'm big enough to cross Las Positas without *you*."

I ran up and snatched her hand right at the corner. I pushed the crosswalk button and made her wait for the little walking guy while the cars buzzed past us on the huge four-lane road. My heart was still beating hard, and the eucalyptus branches were all rattling in the wind, shaking their heads at me, 'cause no way would a knight let his little sister cross that street alone. Mom and Dad hadn't even allowed me to cross Las Positas by myself until I was in the third grade.

I looked back down the hill toward home to see if my friend Ashwin was coming yet. I wished I'd remembered to check the driveway for that old trike. I was pretty sure, even if I had, that the trike wouldn't have been there. But *pretty sure* is never good enough for me.

It never really gets super cold in Santa Barbara, even in January, but something made me shiver. A big brown car with noisy brakes stopped all fast at the crosswalk when the light turned yellow. I yanked Mila back a little, away from the car's rumbling engine, waiting for the light to really turn green before I'd let Mila start walking. I guess I squeezed her hand too hard or something.

"Owwweee," she said.

"I thought you liked when I squeezed your hand."

"No*pe*," she said, smacking her *p*.

I turned around for a sec and finally saw Ashwin running up the hill, dragging his green backpack on the sidewalk. But by then the signal was flashing, and Mila pulled me out into the crosswalk. Talking to Ashwin about those skunks in my driveway would just have to wait, because Mila wouldn't.

She glared down at the pavement, tugged me along, and squeezed my hand too hard right back. But I knew she liked holding it. I knew she wished I would let her hang on to my arm the whole way to school, like I was her old stuffed monkey. But it was only my job to hold her hand when we crossed big streets with stoplights and stuff, and I always did my job. I mean, I mostly did my job. So I smiled at Mila and let her hold my hand as tight as she wanted, because she's my little sister and I'm supposed to take care of her.

I smiled, and she smiled back.

She always did.

She couldn't help it.

3.
The Soccer Ball

I thought about the old trike and those skunks all morning at school.

I didn't have time to say anything to Ashwin about the skunks before the first bell, and Mr. León doesn't let us sit together anymore. He says sitting together makes us "go bananas."

Back in September, Mr. León actually *asked* me to take a spot next to Ashwin, to show him around and stuff, because Ashwin had just moved to Santa Barbara. And it was my first year since kindergarten without a best friend in class, since Johnny Ramirez got put in the *other* fourth-grade section. So it was almost like me and Ashwin were both new. But by October, Mr. León decided that Ashwin was plenty "acclimated" and that we shouldn't talk to each other during class anymore. Even on the way to the pencil sharpener. Now we have a ten-foot rule—Mr. León calls it "buffering the bananas." So the morning after I saw the skunks, Ashwin sat all the way up front at a table with a bunch of girls, and I didn't have anyone to talk to.

By lunchtime, those two weird skunks were riding in circles through my brain, but by then, I wasn't so sure about telling Ashwin about them.

What would he say?

Maybe my story would sound bananas even to him.

At lunch, Ashwin shoved his backpack into the shade under our table. "I've got a good one," he said, his voice all tinny under the metal tabletop.

"A good what?" I asked, still trying to figure out how to bring up the skunks.

"An animal joke, for Mr. León's collection." Ashwin clanged his head on the metal table when he dragged his lunchbox out from under it. "Ouch . . . Why do gorillas have big nostrils?"

"Why?" I was already halfway laughing.

"Because they have big fingers." Ashwin dug around in his lunch like he was searching for a booger.

"No way is Mr. León going to let you put that one up on the bulletin board." I laughed and choked on my juice. Mr. León has two rules about the joke board: the jokes have to be about animals—no people—and they have to be *appropriate*.

"Yeah, I figured he wouldn't." Ashwin shrugged. "But it *is* a good one."

We ate our lunch, waiting for the bell to ring so we could hop up from the hot metal tables. Ashwin told a few more animal jokes, a couple that would probably make the board and a couple that I probably shouldn't repeat. I tried to think of a good skunk joke, but the trike zoomed through my brain until I couldn't concentrate. I decided that once the bell rang and we got away from all the other lunch tables, I'd tell Ashwin about the skunks. It was like a deadline.

Deeeeeeeeeeeeeeep.

The bell rang, and me and Ashwin sprinted for the monkey bars over on the big playground. *Okay,* I thought, adjusting my deadline, *maybe I'll tell him by the last lunch bell.* You have to run fast if you want to stake out the top of the monkey bars. The big playground looks like a huge wooden castle built up against the schoolyard fence. The monkey bars are way on the other end, poking out like a drawbridge. The slides and towers, the swings and hidden tunnels, all connect together, but that stuff is for the little kids.

There are only a few things you can still do in the fourth grade that are really fun. It's cool to play soccer, which I used to do every day, and handball, but that's mostly for girls, and the swings, but those are for the third graders. So sitting on top of the monkey bars and keeping a lookout is pretty much the only thing that's left.

When me and Ashwin made it across the field, a couple of second graders had already started climbing up the slide, which isn't allowed, but second graders are easy to ignore. I hopped up and grabbed the warm metal monkey bars and swung my feet through a gap. When I pushed myself up to the top, squiggling through the open metal square, I was still a little out of breath. This cool breeze blew up from down the hill, and I could see everything: the whole school, the golf course on the other side of the fence, and little snatches of downtown Santa Barbara. The golf course was pretty packed, and its grass looked all green and soft. There's this little cart that drives around and sells drinks on hot days. Might even make golfing worth it.

"I wonder if they sell root beer."

"Bet they do," said Ashwin, kinda drooling. He heaved his backpack up from down below, and I caught it. He's always got cool stuff in there to show me, stuff we maybe, definitely, shouldn't have at school. I was hoping he'd brought a video game. Then a black-and-white soccer ball went whizzing past us—*spish*—and bounced off the chain-link fence between the school and the golf course. I tried to ignore it. I tried to ignore the whole field.

Danny Vega, Gabe Romero, and Johnny Ramirez, who used to be my best friend, were kicking the soccer ball up the field with a bunch of other fourth-grade boys. I didn't see Martin Ortega, but he usually played with those guys too. Last year, I played soccer with them every day.

This September, I figured everything would be the same.

Even though Johnny and I weren't in the same class anymore, we could all still play soccer together, right?

Wrong.

Danny, who likes to pretend to be the guy in charge, said I could play but only on the opposite team, and that Ashwin wasn't good enough *period*, which, no way could he know because he never even let Ashwin try. Johnny only shrugged, so I took Ashwin to see the library. We hung out in there at lunch for a couple weeks before we figured out that staking out the top of the monkey bars was kinda fun too.

Ashwin has only lived here since the summer, and there are a few things about being his best friend that I'm still getting used to. Not playing soccer with all the other fourth-grade guys is one of them. Sometimes I wonder, if Ashwin hadn't moved to Santa Barbara or if my birthday was just a couple of months earlier, would Johnny still be my best friend? Last summer, even before I wound up in the other fourth-grade class, Johnny got a BMX for his birthday and started riding around and doing tricks with Danny Vega and Martin Ortega . I . . . I couldn't keep up. I didn't even have a bike back then. I kind of just ran after them and jumped off rocks. Danny and Martin, dude, they said rude things. Things I can't write down. And I'm not gonna lie, I cried a little.

That day, I could see on Johnny's face that he thought making fun of me like that was wrong.

At first.

"Dude, that was not honorable—no way would a knight say that," I told Johnny, looking away so I could swipe at my face.

Danny jerked his chin at us. "Whatever. How are you even a knight when you don't have anything to ride?" He zoomed away. Martin Ortega rode after him. And Johnny, he rode off with them too.

I tried to shrug it off like Dad always says to do. I didn't have a bike. I got that. Later that day, I asked Mom and Dad to get me one, but I knew they would never buy me something so big unless it was my birthday. Which was two whole months away. Basically forever.

The rest of the summer was weird. Johnny only came over a couple more times, and I only went to his house once. He lives on the other side of the freeway. To get there, all I had to do was walk across this cool fenced-in overpass—it goes over the whole freeway and the train tracks too. But the last time I came by, Johnny didn't ask me to come into his apartment. He only wanted to go ride bikes, and I still didn't have one, so . . . I stopped going over there. But, I don't know, I still thought we were friends.

When I got pushed out of soccer and started spending recess in the library, that's when me and Ashwin really started to *go bananas* together. That's when he became my best friend.

The funny thing is, I don't know when Johnny *stopped* being my best friend. Was it that day with the bikes? Was it the day he didn't ask me to come into his apartment? Was it the day I got kicked off the soccer team? I only know he doesn't come around anymore. Not to my house.

I used to think I understood *everything* about my neighborhood and my school—even my city. When you've got lots of friends, you kinda know where you belong, and things are simple. After all that stuff happened, it didn't feel simple living here anymore, even before I knew I had to worry about trike-stealing skunks. I needed to figure everything out. I decided to start with the skunks. I know it sounds crazy, but I thought that would be easiest to understand.

Watching the soccer ball zig up the field while trying not to think about all the guys who were kicking it was making me dizzy. Ashwin leaned over his lap, playing a video game half-hidden in his backpack.

"What do you know about skunks?"

"Uh . . . they stink. Do we have some kind of a report to do?" Ashwin squinted. "I don't remember Mr. León saying anything about a report."

I laughed and even thought, only for a second, about convincing Ashwin that we had a research report due Friday to see his freak-out face. But I didn't. "Nah," I said. "I just thought you might know something about skunks, that's all. Last night, these skunks . . ."

Danny darted by, his forehead all sweaty, to get the soccer ball.

He must have heard.

"Skunks—yeah, I bet Ashwin knows all about skunks! What's the matter, Mateo? Your new friend farting it up?" Danny said.

Then he made this gross sound with his tongue.

Fpthhhhhhzz.

Fpthhhhhhzzz.

Fpthhhhhhzzzzzzzz.

And the guys on the soccer field laughed. Even Johnny.

"If it gets too stinky up there for you next to that weirdo, you can come play soccer for us. Today. Martin's not here."

Ashwin smiled. Not his real one but the freaked-out smile he gets whenever Danny gives him a hard time. I bet he knew I was thinking about it. Playing soccer. But no way was I going to leave Ashwin hanging there on the monkey bars all by himself. By that point, he was totally my best friend, so it was my job to, you know, back him up. I'd only have played soccer for one day, anyway. Once Martin was in school again, I'd have been out of the game, and Ashwin would've been all ticked at me.

So I ripped a big one.

All those guys heard it.

Swear.

"Nah," I said to Danny. "It's not too stinky up here for me."

I told you I'm supposed to be like a knight. For real. I'm full of honor and loyalty, and I can rip big ones whenever I want.

"Ewwww, zorrillo!" Danny pointed at me, his face a crooked sneer.

The other guys on the field laughed. Johnny laughed too, but it was the good kind of laughing, like I was some funny dude. And besides, they weren't laughing at Ashwin anymore. The other guys all ran off to finish their game. But Danny had gone dark red, like when you wrap a string around your finger and the blood can't get out. He glared up at me, then swung his arms back to pass the soccer ball back in. At the last second, he switched up his aim and threw the ball hard.

Right at Ashwin.

4.
The Library Book

When Danny threw the soccer ball straight at Ashwin, it was like slow motion and fast-forward at the same time. The ball arched through the air. Everything was quiet, and then . . .

Thup.

The soccer ball smacked Ashwin in the nose, knocking him off the top of the monkey bars. Then, *thud*, Ashwin went down into the almost-brown grass. He sat up, coughing. Bet that fall knocked the wind out of him. He grabbed at his nose. There was a little ooze on his hand.

Danny caught the ball when it bounced off Ashwin, kicked it back toward the soccer game, and ran off laughing.

Ms. Printz, the lady on yard duty, was way on the other side of the field. Nobody but Johnny and the other guys had seen. Nobody but those guys ever sees, and those guys never tell. I guess when I hung out with Johnny and them, I didn't tell on Danny either. You just didn't.

Lately, Danny and Martin have been kicking soccer balls at littler kids when they try to sit up on the monkey bars. Danny calls it launching missiles. Whenever Ms. Printz comes over, he and Martin act like it was all a big mistake. So Ms. Printz only tells the little kids not to sit up there. But Danny and Martin had never launched any missiles before when *I* was up there.

Ashwin flopped in the dirt, and I knew there was nothing much I could do. Danny's always been kinda rude, but ever since he got back from winter break, it's been worse. I think he grew an entire foot. He's walking around looking like the Incredible Hulk, ready to explode out of his too-small shorts.

So, no big surprise, he finally exploded.

Not, like, out of his shorts.

Just all over Ashwin.

"Jeez, Mateo. Help me up, man."

Ashwin kept holding his nose, and his words sounded like echoes.

I could tell he was hurt and, maybe worse, embarrassed. I jumped down and took a peek at his nose. It was starting to puff up, and the blood was oozing all the way down into his mouth.

"So gross," I told him, thinking he'd laugh. But he didn't. Ashwin's face was getting all deep red, and I could see him trying not to cry. "Let's go to the library and get an ice pack from Mrs. Deetz—it's closer than the office."

Ashwin let me help him up and nodded, hands hiding his nose again.

"Hey, I thought of one for the bulletin board," I said. "Have you heard the skunk joke?"

"I don fink soh." Ashwin kept talking through his hands, but at least he didn't seem like he was gonna cry anymore.

"You don't want to hear that one." I shook my head. "It *really* stinks!"

Ashwin's shoulders hunched up like a cartoon character. "Ouch—don't make me laugh, it hurts too much," he said.

But I knew he was glad I made him laugh.

It was better than crying on the playground.

By the time we thumped up the metal ramp to the library, Ashwin was still holding his nose, but he looked better than before. He'd wiped a bunch of the blood off his face onto his shirt, and the oozing had stopped.

"Man, Mrs. Deetz is not gonna let me in like this." Ashwin dabbed at his nose with his white shirt again, making the disgusting splatter of blood down the front even worse.

"Just try not to bleed on any books and we'll be fine," I whispered. Mrs. Deetz usually lets kids come in during recess, and you don't have to be as quiet as you'd expect, but I wanted to stay on her good side.

In the weeks when me and Ashwin were hanging out

in the library during lunch, right after I got kicked out of the soccer game, we found this book, *Medieval Weapons and Warfare*, and now we're pretty much obsessed with it. I was already into knights, but that book took things to a whole new level. Right away, Ashwin agreed to be my squire so I could teach him all about being a knight. We probably shouldn't have started with swordplay in the library stacks.

"Mr. Martinez. Mr. Vaz." Mrs. Deetz nodded to each of us when we passed into the cool of the library. She gives me and Ashwin these sideways looks whenever we come in—like, she peeks through her cut-in-half glasses, still typing on the computer. "You both have five minutes to pick your books, and then you will need to take your bananas outside. And before you ask, no, you may not check out *Medieval Weapons and Warfare*. It won't be available until—" She click-click-clicked on her keyboard. "—tomorrow."

After the Swordplay Incident, Mrs. Deetz made up the five-minute rule. I think she and Mr. León talk about us in their teacher meetings or something. How else could she come up with the bananas thing on her own? And then, after Mrs. Deetz set the five-minute rule, came the Catapult Catastrophe. Mrs. Deetz called it that, not me. I think the actual catapult was pretty cool, even if it did get us into a bunch of trouble. But we can't check out *Medieval Weapons and Warfare* whenever we want anymore.

I peeked down one of the aisles. I could *see* the book propped up against Mrs. Deetz's Amazing Engineering display. Even though I thought she would say no, I figured I'd give it a try. All our best ideas, and some of our worst, come from that book. Maybe it would give me an idea about how to track down those skunks. "Come on, Mrs. D," I said. "I feel like me and Ashwin are gonna need the book today, and nobody's even checked it out."

"*Ashwin and I* are *going to* need the book," Mrs. Deetz said.

"Yeah." Ashwin wiped some blood on his shirt again. "That's what Mateo said. But by the time we come back, someone else could get the book."

"Precisely," Mrs. Deetz said. "Someone certainly could check the book out today and use it to get into the same sort of spectacular trouble that you boys somehow manage. Let's give them a chance, shall we?"

"Fine. Can I get the other one then?" I asked. Ashwin elbowed me. "Oh yeah, and Ashwin needs an ice pack."

Mrs. Deetz reached under her desk and took out *Amazing Knights*, my second-favorite book about medieval stuff. She scanned the book with her wand, bop, and handed it to me. "Mr. Martinez."

She swiveled around on her chair and opened the tiny fridge behind her desk. Inside I saw a chocolate milk, about ten jars of iced tea, and a moldy salad. She pulled out an ice pack with little penguins on the cover. "Mr. Vaz," she said, handing over the ice pack. "That looks like quite a war wound."

Ashwin smiled from under the ice pack.

Mrs. Deetz is pretty cool. She never asks dumb questions like, "What happened to your nose?" or "What are you going to do with that book this time?" or "What were you thinking?"

When I checked out *Medieval Weapons and Warfare* the first time, me and Ashwin got pretty obsessed with the catapult page. Building our own catapult was Ashwin's idea, but I'm the one who figured out how to make it. And it was awesome. But Mr. Mendoza, this old guy who lives down the street from school, wasn't happy about that catapult, and neither were his persimmons. Or his cat. Just to be clear, the cat was an innocent bystander and not a target.

When Mr. Mendoza caught us with the catapult, the cat, and that book, he dragged me and Ashwin to my house by our ears. I wish he'd dragged us to Ashwin's house. Mrs. Vaz would have niced Mr. Mendoza to death and promised him all sorts of stuff, and that would have been the end of it. But my mom? She made me write a letter to Mr. Mendoza apologizing for all the mayhem and offering to clean the gooey brown persimmon smudges off his wall, plus a letter to Mrs. Deetz for using a library book in an *inappropriate manner*. Mom even told Mr. Mendoza *he* should write a letter. I don't know what the deal is with my mom and letters.

Mr. Mendoza shoved the book into Mom's hands and told her, "You bet I'll write the school a letter. It's criminal, letting these kids read something filled with such dangerous ideas." Then he pushed his thick, square glasses up on his nose with one finger and marched down our driveway, grumbling.

Mom sighed and sent Ashwin home.

When I gave Mrs. Deetz her letter, I swear she almost smiled. Almost.

"This is the second letter I've received about your Catapult Catastrophe," she said. Her gray hair was like a thundercloud right before the rain, still and quiet and high as the sky. I just stood there, feeling like a squashed persimmon, waiting for her to rain on me.

Deetz wasn't too happy with us, but she didn't make such a big deal about it. No actual lightning exploded out of her head. Now, when we return the book, we have to wait a whole two weeks before checking it out again. She calls it a cooling-off period, which is pretty lame. But other than that, things are pretty much the same.

"All right, gentlemen. You each have what you need, and your five minutes is at an end. I'm sure I'll be seeing you tomorrow," Mrs. Deetz said.

"Hey, Mrs. D," I said. "When do we get to stay in the library for more than five minutes?"

"When you two can make it through those five minutes without knocking something down, telling inappropriate jokes, . . . or bleeding on something." She eyed a couple of new red dots on the blue carpet.

"Thanks, Mrs. Deetz," we said, backing out of the library before turning to stomp down the ramp.

I opened up *Amazing Knights*, which is maybe half as good as *Medieval Weapons and Warfare*, and somebody laughed. I knew it was Danny Vega without even looking.

"Why do you guys keep getting that dumb-ass book? There's no such thing as Mexican knights, weirdos." Some of the guys around Danny snickered. My old friend Johnny pulled at the bottom of his shirt. I flinched a little but kept walking, kinda hoping that the bell would ring so me and Ashwin could go inside.

I know Danny's wrong about the book and about me. I am a knight. And I'm not Mexican—I'm Mexican American. And Ashwin definitely isn't Mexican—he just moved here from Louisiana, and I guess his grandparents are from India. But we are, like, the exact same color brown, and we are exactly the same kind of knight.

We have honor.

Which Danny Vega does not.

Deeeeeeeeeeeeeeeeep.

The bell rang, and all the guys scattered. Some of them were still laughing at us. My shoulders unhunched, and I felt like I could breathe again.

"Come on," said Ashwin. "Let's see if Mr. León will let us put your skunk joke up on the board before social studies."

That's when I realized I still hadn't told Ashwin about the skunks. The real ones. On the trike. I'd missed my deadline. But lunchtime was over, and at least I wasn't Danny Vega's dead lunch meat.

5.
The Knights

Mr. León didn't let us put any of our jokes up, not the one about gorilla boogers, not even the one about the stinking skunk joke, but he laughed at both. "Go sit down, guys—it's time for Mission Studies." He was still smiling and trying not to.

Mission Studies was sort of cool, 'cause our class got to learn about where we actually lived. I had liked social studies last year too—we did a whole unit on the Chumash, the American Indians that lived here before, you know, everybody. But after lunch, concentrating on school was hard no matter what we were studying. I swear, Mr. León sounded like one of the flies stuck between the glass and the window screen next to my table. "Mexico, *buzzzzzzz*, Spain, *buzzzzzzz*, missions, *buzzzzzzzz*, Chumash . . ."

Smack.

I squooshed the fly closest to me against the glass so it would shut up.

Whenever we do Mission Studies, I end up wondering who Santa Barbara really belongs to and feeling like it definitely isn't me. I mean, Mr. León says some Spanish families have been here for hundreds of years. Really. They've got streets named after them: Cota, de la Guerra, Ortega, Carrillo, Castillo. I figure they all go to church up at the fancy mission.

When Spain sailed ships to America, after they finally figured out that it was here, they set up all these Catholic churches on the coast to turn the American Indians into Christians. In Santa Barbara, the Spanish built a presidio too, which is like a military fort, and the soldiers were called conquistadores. Our class got to go to the presidio on a field trip. It even has these super-old cannons.

Martin always tries to act like he's a been-here-since-the-conquistadores Ortega. I don't buy it. I'm not gonna lie, it sounds pretty cool—having a street named after your family. But that's not me. I mean, that's not my family. We moved here from San Diego when I was a baby, and there are no streets named Martinez.

For a while, I thought that's why Danny was so rude and Johnny stopped being my best friend. Because they'd figured something out about me. Like that I didn't belong here. I mean, I don't even speak Spanish. I don't think that anymore, but I still don't get why they have to be such jerks about everything.

Danny says he was born in Santa Barbara and that he and his mom went back to Mexico to live with his grandma until he was five. Ashwin doesn't believe that. He thinks maybe Danny's mom got deported, which is a word Mom had to explain to me, and so Danny had to go with her. If Ashwin said "deported" to Danny's face, though, Danny would probably throw another ball at Ashwin's nose. And maybe I wouldn't blame Danny. It's not the kind of word you can say on the playground.

For a while, I worried about stuff like that. Like, could my parents get taken away? Then Mom explained that since she and Dad were both born in San Diego, that could never happen to us.

"What about Johnny's parents?" I asked. She didn't have an answer for that one. So I just try not to think about it.

I decided to think about something else.

I decided to think about the skunks on my old trike.

What I couldn't decide was what to *do*. It's impossible to think, really think, in a classroom. I needed to get out of there.

When the last bell finally rang at three, I jerked out of my seat, banging my shin on my own desk. I didn't even care. I snagged my homework in my backpack zipper too, but I was the first one in line on the way out the door. I wanted to figure out what was happening with those skunks pretty bad. I still couldn't remember if the trike had been in the driveway that morning—I was twitching to go check. I'd bring Ashwin along and show him too.

I bolted down the hall, heading for the big glass doors. Kids were already pouring down the front steps and scattering off into the neighborhood.

"Slow down, Mr. Martinez," Mr. León called after me. "You need to head to after-care."

My sneakers squeaked on the linoleum.

I forgot about afterschool care.

Again.

After the Catapult Catastrophe, our parents wouldn't let us roam around the neighborhood until they got home from work anymore. We had to stay on school grounds, just like Mila.

I gave the school doors one last look, then ran back down the hall to catch up with Ashwin at afterschool check-in.

"Walk, Mr. Martinez!" Mr. León eyed me all the way down the hall. There was the tiniest flicker of a smirk on his face. He closed his door, and I started running again.

Out in the courtyard, I bumped into Ashwin at the back of the line.

"Walk, Mr. Martinez!" Ashwin said, just like Mr. León would have, with the same half-hidden smirk.

When I got to the front of the line, I wrote my name all messy at the bottom of Mr. Rocklin's list.

Mr. Rocklin runs the elementary afterschool care. Thankfully, the kindergarten kids have their own thing. After-care is always the same: craft table, snack table, the dungeon (that's what me and Ashwin call the multi-purpose room), or something Mr. Rocklin likes to call *active play.* You'd think active play would involve the playground. It doesn't, though. Mr. Rocklin is always digging weird equipment out of the back of the storage shed or trying to teach us some goofy game. But me and Ashwin are in fourth grade. No way are we playing duck-duck-goose. As long as we don't make fun of little kids, accidentally knock over the glitter shakers, or make too much noise in the dungeon, Mr. Rocklin kinda lets us just hang around. Me and Ashwin plunked down at the end of the craft table and scooted some of the art junk out of the way. Mr. Rocklin waved at us with his hands full of glitter, smiling at everybody. The little kids *love* him 'cause he can draw and he'll turn the long jump rope forever, but he never lets me and Ashwin use the playground "unattended." Even when the playground's just sitting there, empty.

"Come on, Mr. Rock," Ashwin said. "Can't we just go over for five minutes?"

Mr. Rocklin didn't even answer. He pointed to a pile of stuff he must have dragged out of the shed for *active play.* A heap of bent Hula-Hoops and a tangle of jump ropes. Ashwin sighed and spread his arms across the table, bonking his forehead on purpose. "So boring," he said.

I laughed a little under my breath. You would too if you'd ever seen Ashwin try to Hula-Hoop. He always bends his knees and bugs his eyes out like a giant, frustrated frog. But I didn't say anything.

I was thinking, trying to remember *everything* about the night before, trying to figure out if seeing those skunks was a dream or what. Ashwin pulled out his video game and played it under the table. I didn't mention the skunks. I kept pushing my deadline to tell Ashwin forward, because my story was gonna sound so crazy. If I tried to whisper it across the craft table, I knew Ashwin would say "No way!" or he'd start laughing and then Mr. Rocklin would come over. Nobody wants that. So I had to wait, even if I felt like the secret was going to jump out of my mouth at any second.

"Are you okay, Mateo?" Mr. Rocklin finally asked, staring at me from the end of the table.

"Yeah, fine," I mumbled, sliding a sheet of paper out of a pile. I picked a marker and doodled until Mr. Rocklin stopped staring. After a while I gave in to my boredom and did some math homework, but I still couldn't get those skunks out of my brain. If you stare at a page of math problems long enough and let your eyes go all blurry, guess what you see?

Skunks.

When we finally signed Mila out of afterschool care and started home, I rushed Mila past Oak Park, even though the mango lady had her rickety wooden wagon set up next to the guy selling ice cream from the rolling cart with the bell.

Ting-ting—ting-ting-ting!

"Mateo, do you have two dollars? Do you have two dollars?" Mila said. She's this tiny thing, but she can suck down a whole mango on a stick with peppers and lime before we even get home.

"Nah," I lied, tugging her down the sidewalk. "Besides, Mom says I've got to stop buying you those on the way home. Spoils your dinner."

Mila scrinched her eyes at me, but that thing I'd said about Mom not wanting me to get mangoes for her anymore was true, and she knew it. Besides, after Mila saw some homeless man taking a leak into the creek at Oak Park, Mom didn't really want us playing there by ourselves anyway.

Once we were past the park, I checked up and down the block. No kids. No grown-ups. It was time to tell. "You know my old red trike?" I said to Ashwin. He nodded. "When we left the house this morning—I'm pretty sure it wasn't there! And last night, I think I saw two skunks *steal* it."

Mila kept walking as fast as she could to keep up with us, and I saw her eyes get all big, but Ashwin only laughed.

"You're dreaming, genius," he said, dragging his backpack with one hand. *Chrrrrrr.* The backpack scraped behind him on the sidewalk. One time, he dragged his backpack all the way home, and when he got there, he realized he'd worn a hole in it and all his homework had fallen out. He's got a bunch of duct tape on the bottom now, and he only lets it slide for a minute before swinging it up to check for a new hole.

Chhhh . . .

Chhhh . . .

Chhhh . . .

Kinda annoying, right? Especially when I was trying to convince him to go on a quest with me. I needed him to be serious. I needed him to pay attention.

The dragging-backpack noise is one of the things about being Ashwin's best friend that I was still getting used to. I'm not saying I wished we weren't best friends. Even though I do still miss Johnny sometimes, I *like* rolling with Ashwin. He can think on his feet, even when he's tripping, and he's this walking idea-factory. Being around him is *never* boring. He's a goofy dude and now he's a knight—just like me.

If I was ever going to figure out what was going on in the neighborhood, I needed an ally, a brother-in-arms, a friend who understands honor. That's Ashwin.

So I had to convince him I was telling the truth. Somehow.

6.
The Truth

Well, convincing my brother-in-arms that two skunks stole an old trike in the middle of the night was a little harder than I thought it would be. I kept saying the same thing—"Seriously, we've got to check if it's in the driveway"—and Ashwin just kept laughing. Not at me, but like I was telling another joke. Even *I* knew it sounded like a joke, but by that time, I'd gotten myself pretty worked up thinking about it. So every time Ashwin laughed, dragging his green duct-taped backpack along the ground, I had to remind myself that we were friends and that knights never give up.

Ashwin stopped walking at our driveway and swung his backpack back and forth with one hand. When he bumped it against Mila, she glared up at him but then edged a little closer so he'd bump her again.

"Come on!" I said. "Let's go check—I bet you the trike's not there."

I ran past Dad's work truck, parked crooked on the

street, and up the driveway, past all our old junk, to show Ashwin the spot where I used to keep the trike.

The trike was *not* there.

After getting so worked up, thinking about it all day, I was actually relieved that the trike didn't just magically show up in the driveway. That meant I had been right. That meant I wasn't going crazy. Most of our stuff was scattered along the driveway: Mila's little polka-dot baby stroller. My new bike, Steed. Even our dusty old wagon. But the red trike with the cool horn had definitely vanished.

"See!" I said, finally sure. "Two skunks stole the trike!"

"Did they really?" Mila asked, staring at me crooked.

"Yes! The skunks rode the trike right down the middle of the driveway and turned out onto the sidewalk, and we've got to figure out what they're up to," I said for the fifth time.

Ashwin laughed. Again. "I gotta get home. I have my piano lesson today." He leaned in and whispered, "Good move hiding the trike, but no one is going to believe you. Why do you even care if Mila rides it? You're totally awesome on your bike now."

Ashwin didn't wait for me to answer. He hurried back down our driveway and onto the sidewalk. He only lives around the corner, which is one of the coolest things about being his best friend—I don't even have to ask to go to his house. But that day I wanted him to stay and I *needed* him to believe me.

Chhhh . . .
Chhhh . . .
Chhhh . . .

My ally, my brother-in-arms, had just walked away—
for a piano lesson. He didn't believe me. He thought I
was hiding the trike so Mila would stop riding it. And
he thought I shouldn't care if Mila made it hers.

I looked at my shiny bike, with its own speed-
ometer, and *knew* I shouldn't care. It had taken me
forever to learn to ride Steed. I didn't even want to
try at first. It's not like I was afraid or anything. I'm
just, you know, careful. If I fall down, Dad always
says, "Shake it off, little man," like that's so easy to do.
Personally, I just want to not fall. Danny and Martin
and Johnny do this thing where they ride down the
overpass ramp all fast, trying not to crash into the
fence at the bottom, knowing sometimes they will. I
don't get it. Anyway, Ashwin was right—I am totally
amazing on my bike. So I knew I shouldn't care about
that old trike.

But I just did.

Would a knight stop caring about his first horse if it
was too old to ride? No way! I didn't care if my knees hit
the handlebars whenever I tried to pedal. I didn't care
that I was supposed to let Mila use it. I did, all the time,
but it was still *my* trike.

"Really?" Mila said again, staring at the empty place
in the driveway.

"Ahhhhg! Yes, really!" I pushed her toward the front door.

Then, at the edge of the driveway, I heard a noise in the oleander bushes, almost like someone whispering. Something black flickered behind the branches.

"Shhh, I hear them."

I ran for it.

My sneakers slid at the edge of the bushes, and Mila crashed into me.

"Where? Where?" She hung onto my shirt.

I bent down and peered into the dark space under the bush. My ears felt hot, and I was sweaty-prickly all the sudden.

But there wasn't anything in that dark space.

No trike.

No skunks.

Only an old, torn piece of a black garbage bag.

"I don't see anything," Mila said, letting go of my shirt.

I felt pretty dumb. I knew my ears were turning dark red.

"Eh, I was just kidding," I said, pushing Mila toward the door again. "Skunks only come out at night anyway."

Mila made a face and stomped up the front steps like a little lightning bolt.

"Daaaad," she shouted, "Mateo said two skunks stole my trike!"

"Great," I whispered, clumping up the steps.

Dad stood in the kitchen, eating a sandwich over

the sink. He laughed and told me to stop messing with my sister.

"He did!" Mila complained. "He said two skunks stole my trike. Then he pushed me into the bushes where the stinky skunks live." She leaned forward, pointing at me and looking ready to explode.

"Where did you put your sister's trike?" Mom asked, clicking into the kitchen from the garage.

"It is *not* Mila's trike," I said. "It's mine, and I didn't put it anywhere—two skunks *stole* it."

"Mateo, I am not in the mood. Go get your sister's trike, now." Mom pointed at me with a hand full of mail.

Nobody believed me.

Nobody would listen.

I crossed my arms and glared at the floor. If they weren't going to listen, I wasn't going to talk. So I stared at Mom's work shoes.

Out of the corner of my eye, I saw Dad shrug. His mouth was full of sandwich.

Mom dropped her keys into the bowl with a little crash. She swung her bag down off her shoulder and sighed. "Mateo, go to your room—until you are ready to tell us the truth." She was all quiet and mad. Mom after work is never like Mom at breakfast. She never smiles that smile.

I threw down my backpack.

I slunk off to my room.

I slammed the door.

Glaring out the window at Steed and Mila's dumb pink baby stroller and the empty place where *my* old red trike should have been only made me feel worse. "It's not hers." I thumped my head against the window. I had the trike even before she was born. Before it was my job to hold Mila's hand and walk her to school and keep an eye out and be everybody's little man. Before I had to share Mom.

Before I had to share *everything* I ever got with Mila.

So the trike was mine all the way.

Even if I didn't use it anymore.

7.
The Lies

Getting sent to my room isn't such a big deal. I mean, I've got books and card games and cool junk and stuff. It's just, I sat in my room while my family was out there, you know, doing stuff. And they all thought I had lied. But I hadn't.

Not this time.

I pressed my forehead against the window, staring at the empty spot in the driveway where the trike used to be. Something shook the oleander bushes a little, and I caught my breath.

But nothing burst out of the bushes.

No skunks.

No whispers.

Only wind.

Maybe I *was* wrong.

In the kitchen, pots and pans clattered, and I knew Mom was cooking dinner. The side door smacked shut, and then I saw Dad rummage around in the shed halfway down the driveway. He lugged the hedge clippers over to the eugenias, and I wished I were out there helping him instead of just watching from the window. Pretty soon, leaf bits were flying everywhere. Then Mila clunked down the front steps. When she hopped off the last porch step, her black cowgirl boots came peeking into view. Then the rest of her appeared like some rabbit at the end of a bad magic trick. She did this little *ta-daaa* thing with her hands and then stuck her tongue out when she saw me staring through the window.

Mila ran across the driveway to grab her polka-dot doll stroller and lugged it backwards up the front steps. *Thunk-thunk-thunk.* A few seconds later, I heard her rolling it around in the kitchen, banging into walls.

"Excuse me, miss? Where can I find the tortillas?" Mila yelled. She was pretending her stroller was a grocery cart again.

"Right over there," Mom said. "At the end of aisle five."

"Where's my stool, Mom? I mean, miss."

I sighed, and all the dead flies on my windowsill skittered away.

That stool used to be mine too. Just like the trike.

That empty spot on the driveway, on my own drawbridge, was making me crazy. I *knew* two skunks stole that trike, and I needed to get it back. I needed to figure out what was going on in my neighborhood. My honor as a knight required it.

I flopped down on my bed and tried not to think about being hungry. I could smell my favorite dinner steaming in the kitchen.

Chicken tamales.

And it wasn't even Saturday.

"Mom's doing this on purpose," I groaned and flopped over onto my stomach. I tried breathing through my pillowcase. The stink of drool and old toothpaste filled my nose, but I could still smell dinner. My stomach growled: *Taaaaa-maaaaa-leeeees.*

I knew what I needed to do.

I opened my door and yelled, "I'm ready to tell the truth."

Then, I lied.

"So," said Mom, "two skunks didn't steal your old trike?"

I hung back in the doorway, keeping my toes far away from Mila's out-of-control grocery cart. Mom had on her favorite sock-monkey slippers, but she still wore her work clothes. She stood at the edge of the kitchen, one hand on her hip, waiting for me to answer.

"Excuse me, miss," Mila yelled while she ran over Mom's monkey toes with the stroller. Two oranges came toppling out of the seat and thumped across the floor.

"Ouch, Mila . . ."

Mom gave me a look, this tired and I'm-so-glad-you're-my-grown-up-little-man look, and I almost couldn't do it. Almost.

"No," I lied. "Two skunks didn't steal my old trike." I stared at the monkey heads on her slippers instead of her face.

"Thanks for telling the truth, mijo." Then, after a long sigh, she added, "So where did you put the trike?"

"I didn't put the trike anywhere," I said. That was the truth. "I don't know where it is." That was kind of the truth.

"Mmmm-hmmm," Mom said. "Go set the table, please."

I slunk across the kitchen and took a stack of plates from the shelf.

"He knows, Mom! He's lying." Mila shook an orange in her hand.

"I. Don't. Know. Where. It. Is. *Honest.* But somebody probably did steal it," I said. The plates felt heavy in my hands. "And it's *mine*," I mouthed to the plates.

"Mateo . . .," Mom said, shaking her head. She took a deep breath as Mila rolled over her slippers again. I waited for Mom to say something else, maybe even send me back to my room, but she didn't. Mila zoomed around me with her stroller, singing, "Mateo knows . . . Mateo knows . . . Mateo knows."

"Mila, it's time for dinner. Take your cart back outside, and put those oranges away. The store is closed." Mom gave me a little smile, just for a second. "Mateo, go tell your dad dinner is ready," she said.

I stuck my head out the side door and yelled for Dad.

He came in from the driveway, covered in little leaf bits. I waited for him to say something about the skunks—he must have noticed the trike wasn't out in the driveway—but he didn't even ask about the trike.

The house phone trilled. Mom rolled her eyes at the caller ID. "Mateo, it's Grandma Martinez. Tell her we're having dinner, okay? My hands are a little full." She *did* have the dish of steaming tamales in her hands, but everything else was pretty much ready.

I ran to the phone and skidded to a stop, bumping into the kitchen counter.

I picked up the phone and booped it on.

"Hi, Grandma—we're about to have dinner."

"Hola, mijo. ¿Cómo te fue hoy en la escuela?" Grandma's voice was always scratchy, like she had a cricket caught in her throat.

"School was fine, Grandma, and you know I don't speak Spanish, and it's dinnertime."

Dad snatched the phone from me. "Hola, Mama," he said puffing his cheeks at me. I think he's kinda scared of Grandma. But I'm not. She gives me money to buy candy when we go see her at Christmas. I just don't like how she's always trying to talk to me in Spanish. She seems so disappointed when I can't answer her back, which is *most* of the time. Trying to speak Spanish makes me feel like I'm doing it wrong, and I hate that. But not speaking Spanish in Santa Barbara seems wrong too, so I'd rather just not think about it.

Dad talked to Grandma Martinez in Spanish for a few more minutes, and then we all sat down.

Dinner.

Smelled.

So.

Good.

Tamales are the most perfect invention on the planet. Maybe even more perfect than my catapult. But all through dinner, Mom kept raising her eyebrows. Watching. Waiting. It was always like this when I lied about something. She just knew. She would sit and wait until I confessed. Only this time, I couldn't. I had no idea where the skunks took my trike.

Mom stopped raising her eyebrows at me across the table and took this deep breath. "Did anything happen today, Mateo?"

Before she could finish, I rolled my eyes. Like, hello, I've been trying to tell everyone! Two skunks stole a trike out of our driveway.

Mom kept at it: "Anything at school, I mean?"

I stared at my plate, thinking about Danny launching that soccer ball right at Ashwin's nose, about him calling us weirdos, about Johnny laughing. I didn't mean to start crying.

I swallowed a bunch of times, thinking I could stop the tears, suck them back in.

Dad leaned over and put his hand on my head, which I know was supposed to help but just made it worse.

Knights are not supposed to cry. Right?

Mom scooped Mila up, and they went into the kitchen to get dessert.

Dad scooted my chair closer to his—*screeech*—and waited.

Mom and Dad both know Johnny stopped coming around our house. They both know we're not really friends anymore. But I'd never really explained about Danny and the stinky stuff he said. I swiped at my face. "Danny Vega keeps saying me and Ashwin can't be knights, and he won't let us play soccer on their team, and today he pegged Ashwin in the face with the ball. On purpose. For no reason." I said it all at once without taking a breath.

I heard Mom slam the refrigerator, mumbling something about macho nonsense. Mila turned the mixer on super high to make the whipped cream, and I couldn't hear what else Mom said. Then Dad did this kind of explaining when he looks me in the eye and his voice gets low and growly—not mean, just deep. He said the macho stuff—Danny hogging the field and being all rough—wasn't nonsense. He said what Danny did was wrong, but it wasn't *all* wrong.

"Bet you Danny thinks he's protecting his territory and his friends. You know, doing his duty, like you do. He thinks he's got to be all tough about it. Bet you he's thinking Ashwin took you over a little. He's probably just sticking up for Johnny."

"No way," I said, getting a little worked up again, "that's not how it is *at all*. And what about Johnny? He's the one who should be sticking up for me."

Dad put his hand on my back, and even though it was sweaty, his hand felt good and heavy resting there. He didn't say anything for a while. "Johnny's still your friend too, you know. But Danny's mama and Johnny's mama are friends, and Johnny's dad works on Mr. Vega's crew. That stuff's important."

I didn't say that I already knew that, but I did. Dad's got a crew of his own, so I know how that works. It's like that with kids too. If your dads work together, you're just in. If your moms are friends, you can always play. It's automatic. Well, Mom and Mrs. Ramirez have never been friends. I mean, they're nice to each other and everything, but Johnny's mom still doesn't know much English. Even Dad has trouble talking with Mrs. Ramirez. He says she speaks Nahuatl, but it sounds like Spanish to me. I already knew all this stuff. I just didn't know why it all had to add up to me losing Johnny.

Dad cleared his throat, and I wiped my face on my shirt.

"Okay, I get it," I said, even though that was kind of a lie. "They're still being jerks, though."

In the kitchen, the mixer finally stopped. "Yeah, I think that's maybe what your mama was saying a minute ago," Dad said.

I laughed, and Dad took his hand away. He kissed

the top of my head, and my back felt sweaty but cool where his hand used to be.

"I'll talk to Mr. Vega. Try to get those guys to give you some space. Some respect."

I knew my dad would. He always does what he says. He doesn't lie.

Well, I had. I lied to Mom when I told her the skunks didn't take the trike, and I lied to Grandma when I said school was fine, and I lied to Dad when I said I understood all that stuff about Danny and Johnny. I fiddled with my fork, clinking it against my glass of milk until Mom sighed. Two skunks riding off into the night on an old red trike was weird, but right then, I thought it would be easier to figure out than not being friends with Johnny Ramirez anymore.

So what if I did lie, I thought. *I'm going to find out the truth about that trike.*

And I'm gonna do it in the middle of the night!

8.
The Internet

After I finished dessert—whipped cream and fruit salad—I made a decision. Before my night watch, I was going to need to do some research on the enemy. Not Danny Vega. The skunks.

I stared down at my empty plate and tried to think of everything I knew about skunks, which was pretty much nothing. To face the skunks and get the trike back, I had to find just the right weapon. Lances were for tournaments, and this wasn't a game. Swords seemed a little extreme, and Mom always says no when we're at the toy store, so I didn't have one anyway. My homemade catapult had been really cool, but Mr. Mendoza was *never* giving that back. I mean, he still had a bunch of oozy-orange polka dots dried on his back wall.

If my house was the castle, then our driveway was the drawbridge, and I was going to guard it. All night. I just didn't really know how. If you want to be a real knight, you have to have a plan, but I had run out of medieval ideas.

"Mom, can I use your laptop? I have some, uh . . . research to do." I pushed my plate away.

"Mmmm–hmmm," said Mom. "Something for school?"

"Yeah, sort of." I scooted back from the table.

Mom raised her eyebrows again, waiting for more, but I just stood there by the table, rolling onto the outsides of my sneakers.

"It's under my work bag." Mom pointed to the pile of things by her purse. "But finish your milk first."

I gulped my milk down so fast that I choked a little and some squirted out my nose. Dad and Mila laughed—they always do—but Mom tried to ignore it. She nodded when I was done, and I squeaked across the room and swiped up her laptop before she could change her mind or Mila could complain about it not being fair.

Last summer, Dad let Mila play some stupid Internet game on Mom's computer, one where you get to design your own pony. I guess Mila deleted something important. Mom got that quiet kind of mad. I think she was mostly mad at Dad, not Mila. She asked how he would like it if she let us play with all his tools and stuff, which was kind of a dumb thing to say, because that's Dad's only idea when Mila and I are bored. We help organize his tools and clean out the truck—it's cooler than it sounds—and then we go get ice cream.

"I let them mess with my tools all the time," said Dad. "I teach them how to use them right, okay?"

"Fine, but your tools are *your* tools," said Mom. "You don't work for a company like I do, and none of those tools cost a thousand dollars."

That's when Dad left. He slammed the door too. I know Mom went to college, like a fancy one, and Dad didn't. She wears her red Stanford sweatshirt on the weekends sometimes. I think the sweatshirt bugs Dad, 'cause he never squeezes her when she wears it.

Every time I pick up Mom's laptop, I remember that argument. The laptop's pretty heavy. Not as heavy as Dad's saw but heavier than his drill. I bet if you added all my dad's tools together, they'd cost more than the computer. "I bought these myself, little man. Remember that when you pick them up," he always tells me.

All I remember when I pick up my mom's computer is that it made Dad mad. So I don't really like holding the computer when they're watching. But once I got to my room, it was fine. It was pretty cool, actually. I could learn anything I wanted to.

When Mila came in to say good night, she swish-swish-swished across the rug in her fuzzy pajamas and leaned over my shoulder to peek at the screen.

"Mom says it's time for bed."

Her breath smelled like strawberry toothpaste.

"Okay. Good night." I swiveled away from her in my spinny chair and raised my shoulders to hide my skunk notes. Mila can barely read Spot the Dog books, but I didn't want to take any chances.

Mila tugged at my sleeve until I spun back and gave her a kiss. I knew she wouldn't leave without one. Then she swish-swish-swished back to the door.

"G'night," she said.

She didn't close the door all the way.

She never does.

I stayed up really late, reading about skunks on the Internet until my eyes started to sting. After a while, I heard Mom and Dad in the kitchen. They were talking soft, so I stretched out my neck, but all I could hear was *mumble-mumble-skunk, mumble-mumble-skunk.* I snuck up right next to my door to listen.

"I heard something weird is going on over at the Vega house," Mom said. "Their trash cans got knocked over every night last week. Garbage went all over the front lawn."

"Well, that's not skunks," Dad said. "They're not big enough. That's usually raccoons. Or some punk kids."

"On Sunday morning, Mrs. Vega found a big hole in one of the window screens too. She said someone took a tarp and some old ropes from the shelves."

"How do they even know what's missing?" Dad laughed. "If someone started stealing from our garage, we'd never notice."

I've seen the Vegas' garage. Everything is, like, arranged. So Mr. Vega would notice.

"It's not funny, Xavier. What do you think?"

"Oh, come on. Mateo wouldn't steal."

I curled my toes into the carpet, like a cat, and waited for Mom to say something. I mean, if anybody deserved to have trash on their lawn, it was Danny Vega, but I wouldn't do that. Not ever. Too easy to get caught.

"I don't know. First weird things at the Vega house, now this story about skunks and a missing trike, plus all that stuff he's saying is going on with Danny and Johnny . . ."

She really thought it could be me.

The teapot started hissing. Mom's spoon clinked her cup. She was making tea.

Probably peppermint.

I pulled my feet back, peeking down at the little empty spaces I'd made in the carpet.

"Mateo wouldn't steal nothing," Dad said, "and that story about the trike is just like that other junk he's always telling you. He reads too many books, like his mama. Leave him alone. He rode that thing forever. He loved it, but he loves Mila too. The trike will show up if we let him alone for a few days. It's time for him to grow up, but he's gotta do it himself."

I heard them kiss.

Mom walked down the hall, stirring her tea.

Dad started to do the dishes. When Mom first went

back to work, that was the deal she and Dad made. Mom still cooked, but Dad cleaned up, and nobody was supposed to tell Grandma Martinez.

Dad turned his little radio on, the one all splattered with paint, and played it soft. Sometimes he sings, like so bad that the lady next door complains. But he wasn't singing that night.

I slunk back to my chair.

I glared at the computer screen and all my skunk notes.

They *both* thought I hid the trike. And Mom thought all that stuff going on at the Vegas' might be my fault.

All the sudden, this was about more than keeping an eye on the neighborhood. I had to clear my name. Whatever was happening at the Vegas' *had* to be connected to the skunks. I didn't care about a bunch of old junk from the Vega's garage, but I cared about my trike. I was going to get it back, and I was going to make those little skunks pay for getting me in trouble.

When I'd read everything I could find on the Internet about skunks, I was ready to face the enemy. I took the computer back and put it on the counter next to Mom's purse.

"Find everything you need, little man?" Dad asked from the couch.

"Yep." I poured myself a huge glass of water and said good night.

I squiggled under my covers, so Mom or Dad wouldn't

get mad if they checked on me, but I read comics with my flashlight and drank about ten more glasses of water so I would have to stay awake. I kept going to the kitchen to fill up my glass. Dad was watching some movie with exploding helicopters and boats.

"You drink any more of that water, Mateo, and you'll never get to sleep. Go easy, okay?"

"Okay, Dad," I said, trying to look sleepy. Knowing he and Mom both thought I stole that old trike and made up some crazy story made me feel less bad about tricking him.

The next time I got up, Dad was still watching the movie, but he had slumped against the brown couch cushions. When he noticed me, I told him I forgot to brush my teeth and shuffled into the bathroom like I was really tired. I ran the electric toothbrush the whole two minutes like you're supposed to, because I figured it would keep me awake. *Vrrrrrrrrrr*. It's like pushing a lawnmower around your mouth. You can still feel it in your hands when you're finished.

The third time I got up to go to the bathroom, the dishwasher was still running in the kitchen but the couch was empty. All the lights were off. I listened for a second over the little *clink, clink, clink* of dishes in the washer. Nothing. Everybody was asleep.

Except me.

I hurried to the hall closet and collected Dad's industrial-strength, ultra-bright work light. Then

I grabbed a container of leftover tamales from the kitchen—the most perfect bait ever. When I put my shoes on by the door, my heart thumped fast. I slid the deadbolt open with a *click* and stopped to listen.

Still quiet.

It was go time.

9.
The Night Watch

When the door thumped closed behind me and I stepped
onto the front porch in the dark, I shivered a little even
though it was a pretty warm night. Balancing the heavy
light and the container of leftovers in my hands, I snuck
along the driveway, careful not to set off the motion
sensor, which is pretty easy if you know where to walk.
I moved past the trash cans and scattered the leftover
tamales in front of the empty spot in the driveway where
the old trike should have been. Then I sat crouched in
my old red sweatpants and too-thin T-shirt behind the
trash cans and waited.

For a *long* time.

So long that the stars got brighter.

So long my legs started to cramp up.

Soon I was shivering and kind of freaked out. But I
didn't turn on the light. I knew I would need it to surprise
the skunks. I read on the Internet skunks don't see very
well and get confused in bright lights. That's why they

are always getting squashed on the side of the road—they get blinded in the headlights of speeding cars. That's what I was going to do. Not squash them, but, you know, blind them in a speedy attack and then . . . get the trike back somehow. I thought I had the perfect plan.

But every tiny sound made me jerk a little. *Bark. Rustle. Thump.* Then a stray cat screamed somewhere down the street. When my heart stopped beating funny, I took a couple slow, deep breaths.

My nose wrinkled.

They were coming.

There's this jasmine vine that grows right behind the trash cans. It blooms every January. I could smell the skunks even over that white, warm-night winter smell. The first whiffs weren't so bad. Not like when skunks are flat on the side of the road and your car smells for a few miles—just kind of musky, like Dad when he comes in sweaty from work. The smell got stronger—they must have been getting closer—so I held my breath and listened. I heard them rustling through the leftovers. Then this slurpy gnawing noise came my way. Gross! I gripped the light tighter but didn't peek around the side of the trash can yet. I hadn't heard the trike creak up, so if I wanted it back, I was going to have to follow the skunks.

"Think we should appropriate the silver bike too, sir?" someone asked in a squeaky voice.

"Negative," someone else whispered. "Can't use

more than one vehicle unless we figure out how to maneuver them on our own. Besides, we couldn't get the bike without triggering their light again. That was an amateur error . . ."

What the heck was going on? I put Dad's work light down in front of me and leaned out around the edge of the blue recycle bin. I leaned so far forward that I accidentally clicked the light's on-button with my knee. And I saw them. Two skunks, chomping on the tamale bits. The little black skunk stopped munching on my leftover tamale and twitched its whiskers. It did not seem confused or blinded or anything.

"Rotting snail-bait, Sergeant Buggies—we've got a problem!" the little skunk grunted.

The bigger skunk kept chewing for a minute. I thought I really was dreaming or just going totally insane— actually, that's a lie. I didn't have time to think *anything.*

"You know what needs to be done, Nuts," the big one said.

"Yes sir, Sergeant Buggies," the little guy said. The skunk turned around and actually stood on its hands.

A handstand—I am not joking.

It lifted its tail.

"Bringing the stink," the upside-down skunk squeaked.

I picked up my dad's light, trying to shine it in the upside-down skunk's face, and stood there with my mouth open. I mean *wide* open.

The skunk squirted right in my face. In my eyes, up my nose, *in my mouth.*

"Ahhhhhhhhhhhh," I screamed and dropped the light. It went *scrunch* on the concrete, and I knew it was broken. My eyes stung so much I could barely see, and my nose and mouth burned with the horrible smell.

The little upside-down skunk flipped back down to its feet with a wiggle.

"Excellent shot, Nuts," the big skunk said.

The burning in my eyes kept getting worse. I tried to wipe the skunk spray off my face with the sleeve of my shirt. Then I heard the skunks scampering down the concrete driveway. I couldn't let them get away! I opened my eyes, but they stung so much I couldn't keep them open. Every breath I took made me cough and gag.

It was worse than the time Mila found that old Easter egg. Worse than moldy lengua in a container I thought had cake in it. Worse than being in a headlock and smelling Mike Feltcher's armpit.

I lunged forward anyway, scattering bits and pieces of my dad's broken light. The glass crunched under my sneakers as I sped down the driveway after the skunks— or whatever they were. I rubbed my eyes and reopened them just as I was about to trip onto the street. I wasn't sure where they'd gone, so I just ran in the direction I saw them take the trike the other night. I skidded around the corner, hoping I'd guessed right. After half a block,

I saw the skunks ahead of me. They zipped through the crosswalk at Castillo and started scuttling down the far sidewalk, between these bright patches under the streetlights. But they weren't riding the trike.

Skunks under a streetlight.

Disappear in the dark.

Skunks under a streetlight.

Disappear in the dark.

When the skunks scampered into that last dark patch, I lost track of them. They didn't reappear under the next streetlight. I ran faster and kept my eyes on the bright circle where they should have shown up, but they didn't. I was coughing when I got to the spot where the skunks disappeared.

I stopped and rubbed at my watering eyes, spinning around, checking every direction. I looked across the street, scanning up and down the sidewalk. I bent down to peek under all the parked cars. Then, *foopsh* . . . I turned to see the two little skunks burst out of Mr. Mendoza's hydrangea hedge *on my old trike!*

The skunks zoomed up Mr. Mendoza's driveway and then shot onto the path that went through his backyard. I ran after them, and my sneakers made loud smacking noises on the concrete. Too loud for whatever o'clock it was. I skidded to a stop where Mr. Mendoza's garden path started. I knew the path curved through his little "orchard" and emptied out on the other side of the block, right next to Oak Park. But even though it's a shortcut to school, nobody cuts through Mr. Mendoza's yard. Ever.

He's always accusing some neighborhood kid of stealing his fruit. Which I *never* do. I only take the stuff from the ground, like with the persimmons, which doesn't count, but I wondered . . . *Should I do it? Should I go through?*

I had to. I could hear the creak of my old trike shooting across Mr. Mendoza's garden. The skunks had almost slipped through to the other side. They were getting away. If I didn't follow them, I'd never know which way they went.

I stepped one sneaker onto Mr. Mendoza's gravel path. *Crunch.*

His porch light snapped on.

I froze.

"Ahhhhg, geezer farts," I groaned under my breath.

10.
The Pink Polka Dots

I dove into Mr. Mendoza's blue hydrangea bushes in an explosion of blossoms. I know they were hydrangeas because he's always shouting at us kids on the way home, "Stay out of my hydrangeas or I'll call your parents!" Whatever, he basically has two whole blocks of hydrangeas. So what if a few blossoms get knocked off?

I crouched down on the ground, with my nose inches from the dirt, and shook the ruined flowers off my head. Mr. Mendoza's porch light stayed on, but I didn't hear anything. Maybe he wouldn't come out.

Smack!

The screen door crashed against the house. Mr. Mendoza stood on his doorstep in a robe and ratty slippers, glaring across the yard. Maybe he wouldn't spot me. He let the screen door slam shut behind him and lurched across the porch. "I see you out there, you little monster!" He headed straight for the hydrangea hedges.

I had no choice. I had to run for it. No way was I

letting Mr. Mendoza bring me home in the middle of the night, not smelling like a skunk's butt, not ever. I stood up and tore through the bushes in another explosion of blossoms. I thumped down the driveway, and Mr. Mendoza shuffled after me, his slippers scraping on the concrete.

"I see you, you little thug! I know who you are! Get your butt back here right now or . . ."

I careened around the corner of his driveway and out onto the sidewalk.

I ran as fast as I could down the block, hoping I would make it to the street corner before Mr. Mendoza really got a good look at me. Even during the day, Mr. Mendoza can't tell me from Ashwin when Ashwin forgets his backpack. That night, there was no backpack. So maybe he wouldn't know it was me. I ran faster. So fast my ears shook.

I was almost there. Almost home.

I could still hear Mr. Mendoza yelling, but I wasn't sure what he was saying anymore.

At the corner closest to my house, I hopped over the big rock. By the time I made it to our driveway, I was breathing too hard to hear anything.

Was he still behind me?

No way could he run that fast. Mr. Mendoza couldn't even stand up straight. But I knew almost nothing would keep him from trying to get a kid in trouble. If your parents weren't home, he'd still find someone to yell at.

Halfway up my driveway, I stopped and tried to catch my breath. Then I heard his slippers on the sidewalk. *Scrutch-scrutch-scrutch*. I dove behind the trash cans again, little bits of my dad's ruined work light pricking through my sweats when I landed.

The sound of Mr. Mendoza's slippers stopped.

I held my breath.

I couldn't hear anything.

No cars. No steps. No crickets.

Then I heard the *scrutch* of Mr. Mendoza's slippers start up again. He kept going up the block—away from his house, away from my house, still searching. I guess he didn't know it was me. Maybe he thought Ashwin had been the one. Maybe he thought I was that kid who lived over on Bath Street. Maybe.

I waited and listened. Too scared to go back into my house. What if Mr. Mendoza walking away was just a trick? What if he was only waiting for me to make some noise?

After a while, I heard Mr. Mendoza's slippers coming back again. *Scrutch-scrutch-scrutch*. When he got to the end of my driveway, I was sure I was lunch meat. But all of the sudden, he started shuffling faster, like he'd seen something. *Scrutch-scrutch-scrutch-scrutch*. He was gone. I know, 'cause I waited. My heart stopped thumping too fast in my chest.

By then, I felt kinda cold and miserable. I started to realize how bad the night watch had gone. No trike, and for a bunch of reasons, I was definitely in trouble.

Number 1. I stank.

Number 2. My dad's ultra-bright work light was a busted-up mess.

Number 3. Mr. Mendoza was definitely gonna tell somebody's parents. Probably everybody's, until he figured out who I was.

Number 4. No way was I going to be able to explain it all away by saying two *talking* skunks stole the old trike. Anyway, Mom and Dad already thought I took it.

There was only one thing to do. I was going to have to lie to Mom. Again.

I brushed the broken bits of plastic and glass off my pajamas and snuck past the light sensor. I'd almost made it to the front steps when I saw her.

Mila, standing on something, peeking out my window. Mila, in her dumb pink footie pajamas with polka dots. I saw her, and she definitely saw me.

"Reason number five that I'm in big trouble."

11.
The Stink

"Did you see?" I asked Mila.

She was sitting on the edge of my bed, arms crossed, little feet tapping against the mattress.

"The skunks?" she asked.

"Of course the skunks, dummy!"

"Yep! I saw." She nodded like ten times.

"Did you hear them?"

"Hear them what? Are they squeaky? I'm gonna call the little one Squeaky," Mila said, bouncing a little on my bed.

"No . . . I think that one is Nuts."

"Nuts?" she asked, tilting her head.

"Yeah, and the big one is Buggies."

"What do you mean, 'Buggies'?"

"That's the skunk's name: Buggies."

"Buggies is *not* a name. You're the one who's nuts!"

"Aaagh! You sure you didn't hear anything?" I asked.

"I heard you scream like you did when you found

that spider on your toothbrush. That's what I heard."

I shook my head like there was water stuck in my ear. Did I really hear what I thought I had heard? *Was* I totally nuts? Mila was definitely looking at me like I was nuts. "Never mind," I said. "Go to bed, Mila."

Mila kicked her feet against my mattress. "I'm gonna tell."

"I know."

"Why was Mr. Mendoza chasing you?" she asked.

"It's not important."

"I'm gonna tell that too."

"*I know,*" I said. "Now go to back to sleep!"

"You stink," said Mila, hopping off my bed.

"Thanks."

Mila picked up my half-empty glass of water from the nightstand, took a sip, and smacked her little lips. "You're welcome. G'night, Mateo." She put down the cup and padded out of my room in her footie pajamas.

I stripped off my stinky sweats and shirt and stuffed them under my bed, but their stink was still making me want to choke. A few minutes later, I shoved the sweats into the corner of my closet. It didn't help. Everything smelled like skunk.

I didn't care. I went to sleep with my face in my pillow, trying not to think about how I was probably, definitely, in the biggest trouble of my whole life.

I kept falling asleep and waking back up. All night, I had nightmares about running after talking skunks. In my dreams, I always got sprayed and the skunks always got away. In the morning, I woke up with a jerk. Mila's face hovered like two inches from mine.

"What are you *doing?*" she asked.

My legs were tangled up in my sheets. Light slanted into my room from the window.

"I was having a dream," I said, kicking the covers off. "What are *you* doing in my room again?"

"So, I decided I'm not gonna tell," Mila said.

"Why not?" I sat up, and she hopped off my bed.

"Mommy says I'm not supposed to go all around the neighborhood without you. So I need you to help me get my trike back. I have an idea for those little stinkers, but I can't do it all by myself."

I was tired of telling her that old trike was *not* hers. Still, I needed her to keep quiet. "You really won't tell?" I asked.

"Nope. But you have to help me find my trike."

I smushed my mouth into a little crooked line. "All right, but you have to help me too," I said, climbing out of bed.

Mila followed me to my closet doing a little skippy-hoppy dance. "Yeah, yeah, yeah! I'm going to need my own flashlight, and I'll catch both skunks like *fooopsh, fooopsh,* and I'm going to call the little one Squeaky and the big one Stinky."

"That's not the kind of help I mean. Come on, Mila. We have to hurry."

"It still really smells in here," she said, crossing her arms.

"I know. That's why we have to hurry. It's my sweats."

I got down on my hands and knees and dragged them out of the closet. "Go to the pantry and get some tomato soup," I said. "The kind Dad likes with grilled cheese sandwiches."

"Soup? Do skunks like soup? How can skunks drink soup if they don't have spoons?"

"Ahhhg! Mila, just go do it before Mom wakes up! And bring the soup to the garage."

She pattered off to the pantry. I ran through the kitchen and into the garage, grabbing a dustpan and hand broom from the pegboard. I slammed them down on top of the washer, flinched at the clangy noise, and then listened for a minute. The concrete floor was freezing, I was only in my tighty whities, and little chicken dots covered my skin. I could hear Mila shuffling things around in the pantry down the hall, but I couldn't hear Mom. I crossed my fingers and hoped she was still sleeping. I threw my sweats into the wash and clicked the big round door shut as quietly as possible.

Mila came in holding two cans of tomato soup high over her head.

"Found them," she said loudly.

"Shhhh! Good—now get the can opener." I grabbed the cans of soup. "And be quiet!"

She padded back a second later, waving the can opener around.

I opened one can of soup, shaking my hand out when it got tired of turning the dial.

"Here goes," I said, getting on my toes.

Mila's eyes went wide. "Mateo," she whispered. "You're putting it in the washer?"

"Yep," I said, tipping the can of soup into the soap bin.

"*In* the washer?" she asked again.

"Yes," I hissed, putting some soap in too.

"This is a really bad idea."

"I know," I said, pushing the start button. The Internet had already been wrong about one thing, but maybe it would be right about the soup!

Click—the door locked.

Whishhhh—the water started swirling in.

"Come on!" I said, grabbing the dustpan and broom.

Mila followed me out the side door and down the driveway. She held the dustpan steady while I swept up every bit of Dad's broken work light and the smashed tamales. Dad's not much of a noticer—he loses stuff—which ticks Mom off. So I figured as long as I cleaned everything up, Dad wouldn't notice the missing light and I wouldn't get into trouble. Mila and I dumped all the broken bits in the trash and ran back inside. I grabbed the second can of soup.

"What's that one for?" asked Mila, shuffling behind me.

"For me." I slammed the bathroom door in her face.

I stood in front of the sink for a minute, trying to

figure out what I was forgetting. The driveway was clean. My sweats were in the wash. The can of soup was heavy and cold in my hand.

The opener.

I cracked the door open.

Before I could even whisper for Mila, she shoved the can opener through the crack. I grabbed it and clicked the door closed again.

Okay, just so you know, showering in cold tomato soup is really disgusting. I dumped it over my head with my eyes squeezed shut, then shampooed my hair five times. At least I could use warm water for that part.

When I opened the bathroom door again, Mila was still there.

She wrinkled her nose. "It didn't work. You still stink."

Then we both heard Mom's door open.

Click, click, click . . . she was walking down the hall in her work shoes.

Mila looked at me.

"Quick! Go get dressed—we have to get out of here," I said. "Tell Mom we're going to Ashwin's for cinnamon buns!"

I ran to my room. Even without my T-shirt and sweats in there, the place still stank.

The only thing to do was leave the house as fast as possible. I heard Dad walk into the kitchen and turn on the coffee grinder. We had to go!

I threw on some soccer shorts and a fresh T-shirt and

snuck out into the hall. Shoving my feet into sneakers, I snatched up my backpack.

"Come on, Mila," I whispered under my breath, hovering by the front door.

Mila popped out into the hall from her room. She must not have brushed her hair, because it was still flipped up like a peacock's tail, and her shirt was on inside out. I waved her toward the door.

"Bye, Mommy. Bye, Daddy," she said. "Mateo's taking me to Ashwin's for cinnamon buns!"

"Bye, Mom," I yelled, opening the front door.

I'd made it halfway down the driveway before Mila slammed the front door. She ran over in her black cowgirl boots and something in her backpack was *tink-tink-tink*ing with every step. Whatever she had in there was definitely not homework, but I had no time to make her take it back.

"You never take me to Ashwin's for cinnamon buns!" she said, grabbing the straps of her backpack.

"There are no cinnamon buns, Mila. We just needed to get out of the house before Mom smelled me."

"Awwww . . . but I'm hungry."

12.
The Smell of Cinnamon

Ashwin lives right around the corner on Calle Canela, another funny little one-block street. When we got to his yard, I told Mila to wait on the front porch.

"I'll go get him. He might not even be ready yet."

I opened the green front door and walked through the living room. Everything is always way-organized at the Vaz house, and it smells like hot rice, even when Mrs. Vaz isn't cooking. Not the kind of rice my mom makes either. It's this white, skinny kind called jasmine. So I felt kinda rude walking in smelling like a dead skunk, but I knew Mrs. Vaz wouldn't say anything. Once, I left perfectly-stamped muddy shoe prints all over the rug—actually, *rugs*, because there are a lot of them—and Mrs. Vaz acted like the rain outside was her fault. I peeked into the kitchen. Ashwin sat at the counter, scribbling away at his math homework.

"Wait, wait. I'm not ready," Ashwin said. "Anyway, you're early. I was about to call you. My mom made her cinnamon buns. They're almost done."

I sat down on the stool next to Ashwin. He thumped his sneakers on the kitchen island. "Number four is wrong," I told him.

"So what? I'm almost done. Anyway, don't get so close. You smell like Mike Feltcher's armpit."

I was about to tell Ashwin how two skunks really did steal my old trike and they had names and I was probably, definitely, in trouble, when the kitchen timer buzzed. Mrs. Vaz came into the kitchen on her sneak-feet. I almost always smell her before I hear her, because she wears way more perfume than my mom. She took the buns out of the oven, and the whole room started to feel sweet and sticky.

"Good morning, Mateo," she said. "You must have a cinnamon bun detector in that backpack."

She slid two out of the pan and put them on plates. *Clink.* She put one down on the counter in front of me. Little sugary threads of icing gooed down the sides. I licked my lips and nibbled a golden raisin that I'd plucked from the top. The bun was still too hot to eat, so I just stared at it. I put my nose over the steamy part, and when I did that, I almost couldn't smell skunk anymore.

Almost.

"You should bring Mila next time. I always make plenty," Mrs. Vaz added. She sniffed at the air a little, like she could detect some not-cinnamon smell but she couldn't quite figure out where the smell was coming from.

Ashwin smirked down at his homework.

"Mila doesn't like cinnamon buns," I said. "My mom always drives her to school when I come here for breakfast."

"Is that so?" asked Mrs. Vaz, wiping her hands on a dish towel.

"Yeah, Mom," Ashwin said. "Mrs. M always does."

"Then who is that peeking through the screen door?"

Me and Ashwin both groaned. There she was. Mila. Waving at us from outside.

"Why'd you bring Mila?" Ashwin asked while his mom let her in.

"I'll tell you on the way to school—and you are not going to believe it," I whispered, hoping he *would* believe me this time.

Mila scrambled up onto the stool next to me, looking as puffy and sweet as a cinnamon bun. I felt a little guilty for making her wait outside. Mrs. Vaz put a sticky bun in front of her too. Mila picked up the whole bun and stuffed a huge bite into her mouth.

"Did you tell him yet?" Mila asked me with her mouth full.

"Shhhh . . . wait until we're outside. It has to be a secret."

Mila nodded like ten times and took another huge chomp. She didn't even put her bun down between bites. She waved it around in the air, making little hummy noises while she chewed. I ate mine one bite at a time, being careful not to get my fingers too sticky. Ashwin bent over and nibbled his without picking the bun off the plate, then leaned back over his math homework.

"I came up with a good one for Mr. León's collection," he said. "What do snakes have on their bath towels?"

"Dude, focus and finish your homework. We've got something important to tell you," I hissed. "Besides, that one's dumb. Snakes don't even take baths."

"Yef they do," Mila said, her mouth oozing icing. "Emma told me snakes lick themselves just like kitties. It's why they have those long, flippy tongues!"

Ashwin laughed so hard he almost fell off his stool. Even Mrs. Vaz laughed, her back turned, as she poured another cup of chai. Grown-ups let some pretty silly stuff slide if they think it's cute. Normally I would have set Mila straight, but that day, we didn't have time.

"How's that homework?" Mrs. Vaz asked over Ashwin's cackling.

Ashwin hunched over his paper again. "One more problem and we can go," he said.

I peeked again and decided not to tell him number nine was wrong too.

"Finished!" he said.

Ashwin crammed the homework into his duct-taped backpack and zipped the pack half closed. Mrs. Vaz handed him a paper towel, and he wrapped his sticky bun in it and started to walk to the door. Mila hopped down from her stool, stuffing the last chunk of her sticky bun into her mouth.

"Pfanks for da ticky bun." Mila waved with her gooey hand, mouth all full.

"You're welcome, Mila," Mrs. Vaz said.

"Goodbye, Mrs. Vaz," I said, pushing Mila out the door.

We all hurried down the back steps.

"So what's going on?" Ashwin asked once we got to the sidewalk.

"Well, first of all, the Internet was wrong," I told Ashwin.

"No way. The Internet is never wrong," Ashwin said.

"Last night, it was wrong about a *lot*," Mila said.

Then I told Ashwin everything.

Almost.

13.
The Ally

All the sudden, it wasn't so hard to convince Ashwin that I'd gone into glorious battle with two little skunks. I mean, I did smell pretty bad, and Mila had seen them too.

It wasn't even hard to convince him that we had to get the trike back. Our honor required it. Protecting the neighborhood was a duty that we couldn't ignore. And like I said, Ashwin understands about having honor and being a knight. I needed to bring back the trike, clear my name, and make those skunks pay. Ashwin got it. He always thinks my plans are awesome.

By the time we had walked to school, the bell was already ringing, and like I said, me and Ashwin don't sit together anymore, so The Plan had to wait. I picked a book out for Sustained Silent Reading—Mr. León says it's good to start every day with something quiet—and tried to suck in my stink as I walked back to my desk.

I hadn't even opened my book yet when the kids around me started to whisper.

"Stink bomb malfunction," I said under my breath, which maybe wasn't such a good idea. A couple of kids laughed.

"Mmmhrgh." Mr. León cleared his throat. "Come on up, Mr. Martinez."

I walked up to his gray desk, holding my SSR book.

"What's all this whispering about?"

I rolled onto the sides of my sneakers and shrugged.

Mr. León spread his palms on the desk, then fiddled with the handle of the drawer where I knew he kept his referral slips.

My brain started to spin. Did he hear the thing I said about the stink bomb? I didn't know, but I had to say *something*. "I, um . . . Well, Ashwin came up with this new animal joke, only I don't think it's so good. It's, 'What do snakes have on their bath towels?' and the punch line is, 'Hiss and Hers.'" I shrugged. "I like the jokes that are real, you know? Like the gorilla booger joke, but you already said no to that one."

Mr. León took a deep breath in and then sighed.

I was sure he smelled me.

I gave him my best, most innocent face—I learned it from Mila. I mean, maybe Mr. León would think the smell was just some new BO, like Mike Feltcher had. I could totally grow hair under my armpits. Any day now.

Rebecca, this girl who always sits up front, was rolling her eyes and whispering to the girl next to her.

"Rebecca, eyes in your book, please. Mateo . . ." I

swear, Mr. León tried not to smile. "If I get any stink bomb reports from the custodian, you and I will be having a serious conversation." He put his hands back on top of his desk.

"Got it, Mr. León." I nodded and took a step back.

"In the meantime, Mr. Martinez, put it on the board."

"Put what on the board?"

"The joke."

I grinned and walked up to the Animal Joke board. I could feel Mr. León watching me. He didn't actually say which joke to put up. He just said *the* joke, but we'd talked about two. I wrote, *Why do gorillas . . .* and peeked over my shoulder. Mr. León just smirked, so I put the rest up. I made it through the whole morning without any more whispering from Rebecca, and Mr. León never did open that drawer of referral slips.

At lunch, me and Ashwin walked down the row of shiny metal tables, looking for an empty one. Danny Vega, Martin Ortega, Gabe Romero, and Johnny Ramirez were all sitting at the table closest to the dry, yellow-green field. When we moved past them, they all switched into Spanish, which is kind of like a secret language on the playground.

Ashwin threw down his lunch bag on the last empty table, right next to the trash cans. It skidded across the top and slid off the other side and then thumped down onto the hot blacktop under the table.

"Man, I thought I was going to make it that time."

He picked his backpack up and started to unzip the cover of his lunchbox. Blueberry yogurt oozed over the edge of the lid.

He scraped at some yogurt with his sandwich.

Like that was totally normal.

"How do you think the skunks figured out how to ride the trike? Do you think they have a disease? Are they, like, crazy mutants created by toxic waste?" As Ashwin talked, he waved around half a salami sandwich. Then he dipped the sandwich in his yogurt and took a huge bite. Sometimes eating with Ashwin is weird. You kind of have to ignore it.

"Don't know," I shrugged. "I don't even think it was hard for them. They could just ride the trike." I wasn't sure how much to tell Ashwin. He totally believed me already. If I said the skunks could talk, would he think I was joking? I decided to keep that part of the night watch to myself until I was sure what was going on. Anyway, showing him would be easier than telling him.

"So where do you think the skunks took the trike?"

I didn't answer because I saw Danny get up from his table and start walking over to the trash cans. He wadded up his big brown bag and pretended to shoot it like a basketball. It missed the trash cans and thunked down onto the table between me and Ashwin. Little bits of green Jell-O sprayed everywhere. I got some in my eye.

"Whoops," Danny said. "I always miss when you guys are sitting there."

Ashwin squirmed a little. I squinted up at Danny and saw the yard-duty teacher hovering next to the kindergarten kids.

"No problem, man," I told Danny. "I heard you have kind of a problem with trash."

It was a lame line, not my best, but Ashwin laughed and tried to hide his smile. I'd already told him about the mess all over the Vegas' lawn. Ashwin stuffed another bite of soggy yogurt-sandwich into his mouth but had trouble chewing it.

Danny smacked his hands on the end of the picnic table and leaned down over us. Ashwin flinched, and maybe I did too.

I heard some kids at a first-grade table laugh.

"If I find out it was you, you're gonna be sorry, weirdo." Danny needed to brush his teeth, and he was leaning so close I could see the freckle on his nose that was shaped like California.

Martin, Gabe, and Johnny popped their heads up from their lunch table, ready to bring Danny some backup. When Johnny saw me, he started staring down at his lunch. He'd been my best friend for *four* years. I know even more about Johnny than I do about Ashwin. I know he likes stuff that glows in the dark: fireworks, shirts with bones on them, and that cool electric-looking algae in the ocean. I know he's afraid of lizards and loves his baby sister, Noemi, pretty hard. And I know his real name is Juan but only his Mom calls him that. Even though I only saw him at school now, or riding bikes up on the overpass, I knew him and he knew me. So I knew he wasn't gonna come over and back up Danny. Not in a fight with me. But Martin kinda half stood up and Gabe definitely gave me some stink eye.

I leaned back from Danny's breath and saw the yard-duty teacher coming down the row of tables. She was pretending not to watch us, but I could tell she was.

"I don't know what you mean, man. I thought you were practicing trashsketball on your front lawn. Was your mom mad?" I asked Danny, and crammed some chips into my mouth.

"Whatever, weirdo. We put in an alarm. Next time anybody gets near the trash, me and my dad are coming out with baseball bats. And I only miss when I want to." Danny wrinkled up his nose like he smelled something gross, probably me, and the California-shaped freckle on his nose looked like it cracked in half.

Danny was a natural disaster, like an earthquake or a hurricane. You never knew how bad it was gonna be until it was over. Sometimes he would just roll through, shake things up, and maybe knock somebody's hat off. Nobody got hurt. Other times—no warning, nobody watching—*bam*. Major damage. Like with that soccer ball. I don't get why he has any friends left. But I guess, before Ashwin came, I used to just put up with Danny too.

When the bell rang, Danny smacked the table one more time, then thudded off to the soccer field.

He left his wadded-up brown paper bag oozing green goo on our table.

"It was kind of dumb for him to tell us that," said Ashwin. "I mean, if it was you messing with the lawn, that would have been dumb to warn you about the alarm."

"Yeah, Daniel's a real thinker."

We both laughed, and my heart started, like, beating again.

"Let's go stake out the monkey bars," I said.

But before we could get up, the yard-duty teacher came over and pointed to the mess on our table. She didn't even say anything. I think she knew the trash wasn't ours. I grumbled a little under my breath, but I threw away Danny's sticky oozing-green-goo bag anyway.

If I was going to make it through the rest of recess alive, I needed to stay on Ms. Printz's good side.

14.
The Plan

So, the rest of recess didn't exactly go like I planned. Danny and Martin did that thing again. Launching missiles. After one close call, me and Ashwin hopped off the monkey bars before those guys could come over and do any more trash-talking.

We found Ms. Printz to see if she would do anything about it. But we chickened out of blaming Danny and Martin when she asked, "Who kicked the ball at you?" and "Did you tell them how you felt about that?" and "Do you want me to help you talk it out with them?" all in one breath. What I really wanted was for Ms. Printz to send those guys to the office, but she never does, so what's the point in telling?

Nobody else even tried to hang around the monkey bars. It's not like Johnny and those guys even use them. I guess they just don't want anybody to have fun on the bars when they're around.

After that, me and Ashwin didn't really have time to

map out The Plan. By the end of lunch recess, that's as far as we'd gotten—calling it The Plan.

During afterschool care, me and Ashwin told Mr. Rocklin we were going to hang out in the dungeon. No way was I going to spend another afternoon chained to the craft table, staring at my homework. We had stuff to figure out.

"Sure," Mr. Rocklin said, "but if I hear you guys jumping off the stage again, the multi-purpose room will be off-limits."

We snatched up our backpacks and ran.

The craft table is right outside the multi-purpose room, and Mr. Rocklin makes us keep the doors open, but he only ducks his head in to check on us every half hour or so. So it was the perfect place to work on The Plan.

Inside, I blinked. The dungeon doesn't have any windows, and after school, the hanging lamps are switched off. A couple of them are busted anyway. Up front, off to the right of the stage, an old rug, some bookshelves filled with puzzles and dusty board games (which all have broken boxes and missing pieces), and two beanbag chairs lurked in the gloom. Me and Ashwin both sprinted for the red chair, our steps echoing in the big room. I leaped with my arms in front of me and, *spooosh*, landed first.

Victory.

Ashwin landed right on top of me a second later.

"The chair is mine," I wheezed.

Ashwin rolled off and spooshed into the blue

beanbag. (That one leaks these tiny foam balls all over your clothes.) We scooted the beanbags together and stared at the ceiling. A couple first-grade girls came in and started a game of bird bingo right next to us, so we had to whisper. But after I'd answered all of Ashwin's questions like a hundred times, I still wasn't sure how we were going to get the trike back.

"We need to go to the library," I said.

"Ahhh, come on, Mateo. You dragged me there once this week already. Besides, we need to work on The Plan, and how are we gonna learn anything in that place? Mrs. Deetz is probably already all closed up."

"We *will* be working on The Plan," I said. "Mrs. Deetz said we could get *Medieval Weapons and Warfare* today, remember?"

I hopped up out of my beanbag and ran to the dungeon door, trying to peek across the blacktop. I could tell Mrs. Deetz was still over in the library.

"Hey, Mr. Rocklin!"

Mr. Rocklin looked up from the craft table and squinted at me.

"Mrs. Deetz's door is still open—can we go?" I asked, pointing at the other end of the courtyard. At the craft table, some kid knocked over a tub of glue. Before Mr. Rocklin bent over to clean it up, he sighed and nodded at me.

I shouted back into the dungeon, "Come on. Let's hurry before she closes."

Ashwin groaned and heaved himself up from the blue beanbag, swiping off all the little foam balls. The little first-grade girls ran over when they saw Ashwin get up. They pounced onto the beanbags and started giggling.

"Ah, man, now you made us lose our spot. Mrs. Deetz better let us have that book."

I ignored Ashwin and ran across the blacktop to the library ramp. When I walked in, Mrs. Deetz smiled at me from her desk. If you didn't know her, you wouldn't think it was a smile, but I do, and it was. "You go get *Medieval Weapons and Warfare*. It's in the section on building stuff. I'll ask Mrs. Deetz about skunks," I said to Ashwin.

"It's 3:10, gentlemen. You have five minutes to check something out before I lock the library doors," Mrs. Deetz said, standing up with her arms full of books.

"Don't we always only have five minutes?" I asked.

For a second, even though she'd smiled when we walked in, I thought maybe she wouldn't let us check anything out.

Then she said, "True enough, Mr. Martinez. True enough. What can I help you find today?" She put down her stack of books with a *thump*, and I grinned.

Mrs. Deetz found me two books on skunks. I checked out the fatter one.

"There's gotta be something in here," I told Ashwin when he walked up with *Medieval Weapons and Warfare*.

"Doing a little research, are we?" said Mrs. Deetz.

She gave me a double sniff and raised her eyebrows. I just stood there, trying to look innocent.

Mrs. Deetz picked up my book and then Ashwin's. Her computer made that great little *boop* sound as she scanned the book on medieval weapons. Then all she said was, "Happy research, boys—and I hope I won't be getting any letters from angry neighbors this time. These are due back in two weeks!"

We ran back to the dungeon. The first-grade girls were both piled in the blue bean bag (I guess they don't care about foam balls all over their butts) with an origami fortune teller in between them. Me and Ashwin sprinted for the red beanbag with our books. *Spoosh*, we landed right next to each other, but I guess Ashwin's book banged into one of the girls.

"Hey, you smushed my fingers," said one of the girls.

"Yeah, and we were using *both* the beanbags!" said the other girl.

"Were not," Ashwin said, rolling onto his back in the red beanbag. "You were both in the blue one when we came in." He started flipping through his book.

The girl with the smushed fingers looked like she was gonna cry. Her friend crossed her arms, all grumpy.

I checked the bright rectangle of the doorway for Mr. Rocklin. No way was he going to put up with us being mean to the first graders. Mr. Rocklin might not say much, but he's got rules. If I didn't do something fast, we'd be spending the afternoon gluing glitter onto paper plates.

"Hey, come on, man," I said, elbowing Ashwin in our bean-bag. "No squishing the little guys, remember? You said the oath."

Back in October, me and Ashwin both recited this oath of knighthood we found in the back of a book. I wasn't super sure if Ashwin was ready to be a full knight, but Ashwin said he was tired of being just a squire. Anyway, we took the oath:

I shall be without fear in the face of my enemy, withoutmeanness, withoutspite, andwithouttreachery. I shall be brave and loyal, even if it means my death. I shall safeguard the small and helpless with my dying breath.

"What's spite?" Ashwin had asked. "Is that like ye olden talk for spit? Can we not spit anymore?"

We looked up *spite* in the dictionary later. But this thing with the first graders getting squished was more of a "small and helpless" situation.

Ashwin muttered, "Fine. Sorry," to the first grader he bumped with his book—her name's Camila—and he flopped out of our beanbag and onto the rug.

I slunk over to Ashwin, and Camila glared at us the whole time. She didn't seem like she was gonna cry anymore.

"I'm gonna tell Mr. Rocklin what you did," Camila said, going all wiggly. Her friend, Jasmine, nodded a billion times.

"Come on—he said he was sorry," I told them, pushing Ashwin's shoulder.

"Yeah, I am, I'm sorry. I didn't mean to squish you. Swear."

"The beanbags are all yours," I said. "Just leave us alone, okay?"

Camila and Jasmine got a little snorty, but they went and scooted the chairs way off to the side of the rug. They only glared at us a little after that.

I opened my book on the worn rug. Ashwin was already thumbing through pages of *Medieval Weapons* again.

"Oooh, cool—check this out! Do you think we should build a siege tower?" he said.

"Ashwin, they're not hiding out in a skunk castle," I laughed, bending back over the skunk book.

"Fine. But we should try that next time Danny Vega has a sleepover in his tree house and won't invite us."

See? Ashwin's a total idea factory. You flip a switch and he hums along like a machine, spitting them out. Good ones. Bad ones. Crazy ones. Amazing ones. Sometimes it's hard to tell which ones are the bad ones until you try them out, but I filed the tower idea away for later. We had work to do.

The first thing I did with my fat skunk book was peek in the index for the word *talking*—nope, not there. Then I searched for *speaking*—not there either. So I started reading the skunk book from the beginning. It was all pretty much the same stuff I read on the Internet. *Spotted skunks are secretive and crafty creatures, blah, blah, blah . . .* No kidding. I was getting pretty frustrated. Then I read, *Skunks make a variety of vocalizations that include hisses, growls, squeals, and cooings.* That was definitely *not* what I had heard. Maybe I'd just been really tired the night before. Maybe I was going crazy. I decided I definitely shouldn't tell Ashwin that I thought the skunks could ride trikes *and* talk.

"What about a death trap?" said Ashwin. "We could dig a hole and attract them to it and when the skunks ride over the hole on the trike—*crunch!*"

"Nah . . . that would ruin the trike." I shook my head.

Ashwin gave me that why-do-you-care-anyway look, and I stared him down.

"Okaaay . . . no death trap," Ashwin said. He flipped to a picture of some soldiers dumping hot oil onto a drawbridge.

"Let's switch books," I said. "There's got to be something in here somewhere," I mumbled, skimming through *Medieval Weapons.*

"Listen to this," Ashwin said, getting excited. But I was only halfway listening, because I was getting an idea. "It says, 'The smell of a skunk can deter a dangerous predator.' I totally believe it. You still reek."

"That's it," I said, staring down at the weapons book. "That's exactly what we need."

"A dangerous predator?" Ashwin asked. "Yeah, that

would be cool. But where are we going to get one?"

"No, Ashwin," I said, holding up my book. "*This* is what we need."

"Armor?" he asked.

"Yep. Skunk-proof armor."

15.
The Armor

Right at 4:30, me and Ashwin hustled over to the kindergarten classroom where Mila has her afterschool care. Mom signed a special form so I'm allowed to check her out all by myself. Kindergarten afterschool care is this land of miniature chairs and short toilets—the kids even have their own tiny playground out back. I can't believe it used to look fun to me. When we walked in, Mila was asleep in the fuzzy chair by the bookshelf. She had an open book in her lap, and her head was flopped to the side. Her hair was even puffier and more tangled than it had been that morning. It was kind of cute.

"Hey, Peacock Head," I said. "Wake up."

She wriggled in the chair, opened her eyes, and wiped a little trickle of drool off her cheek. I was feeling kind of tired too, but I was so excited about The Plan that my head had that buzzy feeling you get before your birthday party or Christmas.

"I'm ready!" Mila hopped out of the chair. "I'm all rested up for tonight."

"Tonight?" asked Ashwin.

"Yep!" Mila said. "You know. We're gonna catch the skunks and get my trike back. Tonight." She zoomed across the room and took her backpack from the row of metal hooks.

"She can't spend the night, Mateo," Ashwin said. "No way. And if we spend the night at your house, your mom will know we're up to something. She always does."

"That's because, when you come over, we always are," I said, shrugging.

"Anyway, Mila can't come."

"I know. I'll tell her," I said. "But she's not gonna like it." I signed Mila out at the door. She grabbed my hand and tugged me along before I had time to grab my backpack straps. When we got to the sidewalk, she started skipping, bobbing like a helium balloon at the end of my arm. As we passed by Mr. Mendoza's, I caught him watching us from his window and I tugged Mila along a little faster. He hunched over, pushing his face close to the window. His thick, square glasses almost touched the pane. I didn't think he *knew* it was me the night before, but I could tell he thought it might be. Once we were past his house, I slowed down again.

"Mila, you can't come tonight," I told her when we were almost to our driveway.

She stopped. "What do you mean? You said you guys were going to come up with The Plan!"

"We did."

"Yeah—we totally did," Ashwin said. "It's gonna be so cool!"

"We have to spend the night at Ashwin's tonight or The Plan won't work. If Ashwin comes to our house, Mom will catch us. And no way can you sleep over at Ashwin's. Then Mom will *definitely* know something is up."

Mila glared up at me and crossed her arms. She had trouble staying angry and walking at the same time, though. So she had to grab the straps of her backpack and hurry to catch up.

"But you guys, I have a plan too. I could be your backup. Mom says you always have to have a backup plan." Mila was out of breath.

"Shhhh! Keep it down, Peacock Head. Do you want the whole neighborhood to know?" I put my hand out in front of Mila and peeked around the bushes along our driveway. Mom's car wasn't there yet, but some Fridays, she came home early. Dad's work truck wasn't parked on the street either, but we probably only had a few minutes before he got home. Anyway, we would hear Dad's truck before we saw it. The fan belts always screamed.

I took one more look down the street for Mom's car.

"You can *help* with The Plan," I said to Mila, giving Ashwin a nod over her head.

"How?" she asked.

"I can't go inside smelling like this—Mom and Dad might catch me when they get back. And we need some stuff from the house. So you go grab the supplies, and I'll call Dad from Ashwin's house. All you have to do is bring all the stuff to Ashwin's—you won't even need to cross the street. How much do you think you can carry?"

Mila cocked her head to the side. "I can carry *anything.*"

I bent down and whispered the list of stuff we would need into her ear. Ashwin rolled his eyes at me while he waited. "And don't let Mom see you with any of that stuff," I told her. "You have to find it right now, before she comes home."

"Okeydokey." She put her hands on her backpack straps again and started to march down our driveway.

"Better hurry!" Ashwin added.

Mila started to run with her backpack shaking on her butt, and whatever she had in there was *tink-tink-tink*ing again.

I grabbed the handlebars of my bike, Steed, and we ran with it down the driveway.

"I still don't see why we need to ride our bikes tonight," Ashwin said, panting next to me.

Ashwin only had his older sister's funny looking banana-seat bike to use. He hardly ever rode it. He hated it. His sister was way older and didn't care if he borrowed the thing. But Ashwin cared. Once, Danny

Vega saw him riding it around down by Oak Park and gave him a pretty hard time. I mean—it's a *girl's* bike. It even has a basket on the handlebars with plastic flowers all over it, which Mrs. Vaz wouldn't let Ashwin rip off. Mrs. Vaz makes great sticky buns, but she has no idea when it comes to bicycles.

Even after I finally figured out how to ride my new bike, Ashwin didn't really ever want to go out with me and ride around.

And I didn't blame him.

"Don't worry about it," I said, keeping an eye on the street for Mom's car. "The skunks were too fast for me last night, but they'll never get away from us now. Besides, it will be dark, and Danny Vega won't see."

We were almost to the corner, but Ashwin still seemed nervous.

Remember what I said about Danny being like an earthquake?

Sometimes he rumbles in before you even know he's coming.

Right then, I heard the clicking of bike gears behind us.

Scrich.

Scrutch.

Scrooch.

Three bikes braked around me and Ashwin. Danny and Martin and Johnny must have been looking for us, because they usually never came that far past the park. I thought at first that Danny had decided all that trash on his lawn really was me and he was here to make me pay. But I was wrong.

"See," Johnny said to the other guys. "He's got a bike now—so he can roll with us." It had been a while since Johnny and me had talked. His voice sounded the same, I guess, but something felt different.

Ashwin smiled his freaked-out smile. He was the only one not standing with a bike, but right then, he was probably glad about it.

"Cool bike," said Martin, nodding to Steed.

"It's all right," said Danny. "Can you do any tricks?"

I shrugged. "I'm working on a couple things," I said. Which was a lie.

Johnny grinned at me. He knows me the best of all those guys, so he probably knew that thing about the tricks wasn't exactly true. "Let's go down to the overpass—I'll show you how to pop a wheelie," he said, nodding in the opposite direction of Ashwin's house.

Ashwin's freaked-out smile got bigger while he waited for me to answer.

Johnny gave me this look, this asking-me look. And I thought about it. Johnny was right. I did have a bike now. I could totally roll with him and Martin and Danny, just like I used to. I even kind of wanted to. A little. But I figured I would probably have to stop calling my bike Steed—I knew what Danny would say about that. And then I thought about trying to explain to those guys about what was going on with the skunks, about The Plan, and my idea for skunk-proof armor. They'd just think I was lying. About all of it. I knew they wouldn't believe me like Ashwin did. Especially not with Danny around.

"Come on, Mateo," Johnny said. "Popping a wheelie isn't even hard. Ashwin doesn't have his bike, right? I don't know—you could catch up with him later or something."

"Or never," Danny said, making Martin laugh all quiet.

"Nah," I said. "Me and Ashwin are kinda doing something."

"Told you," Danny said, putting one foot on a pedal. "Bet you he can't even ride that shiny bike. Why are you walking it, anyway? You scared to fall? Let's go—this is boring."

Danny hopped onto his bike and zipped in between me and Ashwin, knocking Ashwin out of the way. Martin zoomed after him, snickering, and they both jumped a curb. Johnny stood there with his asking-me look. "Come on, Mateo—we'll have fun. You gotta come. I can't keep backing you up if you don't roll with us," he said, grabbing his handlebars tight.

And that, that right there, made it easy. Or easier. He never really did back me up, I thought. Johnny didn't kick balls at us or say rude stuff, but he didn't really stick up for me or Ashwin. Not ever. Johnny knew all about me, and I knew all about him, but I didn't understand him anymore, and he didn't understand me. Johnny didn't get why I had to defend Ashwin, my brother-in-arms. But me and Ashwin had said an oath. Together. I still liked Johnny. Wanted to be friends, even. Just not without Ashwin.

"Nah," I said again, staring right at Johnny. "Like I said, me and Ashwin are doing something." Ashwin's freaked-out smile disappeared. His real, goofy, ready-to-go-to-battle-by-my-side smile came back.

"He could come over too, Mateo. That's cool with me," Ashwin said.

Johnny tugged at the bottom of his T-shirt with one hand, which I know he does when he's nervous. I chewed on the inside of my cheek, waiting for him to say something.

Danny and Martin skidded to a stop at the corner. "Come on, Johnny. You coming or what?" yelled Danny.

Johnny kicked at his pedal a couple times, then told me and Ashwin, "Nah—that's okay. We're doing something too."

And Johnny rolled away.

Back in September, when I'd taken Ashwin to the library instead of playing soccer at lunch, I hadn't really known what I was doing. I didn't get that I was choosing sides.

That day, I did, and so did Ashwin.

And I also knew it was time to talk some trash.

"Man, Danny thinks he's so cool 'cause he has a backyard and got to build his own tree house. 'Cause he speaks Spanish and goes to Mexico at Christmas for like the whole month. 'Cause he comes back with piles of spicy candy and only shares it with Johnny. But no way is Danny Vega a knight."

"Not even a dark one." Ashwin grinned.

"Let's roll," I said.

We both ran—me pushing my bike and Ashwin checking over his shoulder to make sure those guys were gone. I still don't really know how to explain what it felt like. We'd come within inches of Daniel Vega without getting squashed. I bet you my dad had said something to Danny's, and that was a relief, but Johnny had rolled away, and this time I knew he wasn't coming back. I couldn't feel mad at Johnny about it, but I could still feel mad at Danny—not for me, but for Ashwin.

We turned the corner to Ashwin's house, and I relaxed. "After we get the trike back, we should ride our bikes through Danny's garden," I said. "I bet you they don't have an alarm on that."

"Yeah," said Ashwin, smiling with his mouth open. "And I'll run over that *KEEP OUT* sign next to his junky tree house!"

Me and Ashwin laughed and ran down his driveway. I leaned my bike next to the rusty orange girl's bike back by the garage. Ashwin hadn't ridden it in such a long time that little bits of ivy were growing over it. When we got inside, I called Dad and left him a message while Ashwin raided the fridge. He spread blobs of peanut butter and jelly on spicy cheese puffs. He smushed them into little worm sandwiches and ate them one at a time.

"How can you eat that?" I asked.

"Come on, try some. It's sooo good." Ashwin opened his mouth wide so I could see everything.

"Gross," I said, snatching the last sticky bun from the pan.

Out the kitchen window, I saw Mila zooming up the driveway. Her polka-dot baby stroller was overflowing with stuff.

"Here comes Mila," I told Ashwin.

"Already?" he asked. "How did she get all that junk you asked for?"

"It's not junk," I told him. "It's our armor!"

Mila rammed the doll stroller into the back steps, and my fireman rain boots came shooting out. They landed on Ashwin's back porch—*thump, thump.*

"Your stinky sweats were already in the dryer," she said. "Dad must have done it. So I brought those too."

I sniffed at the clothes. They did still stink, but only a little. Mostly they smelled like all the soap I'd dumped in the washer and a little bit like tangy tomato. I guess Dad didn't notice, so I must not have busted the washer.

Me and Ashwin unloaded all the stuff from the stroller and hid everything in the bushes by the back steps. We were almost ready!

"I figured it out," Mila said. "I know how we can catch the skunks."

Ashwin gave me another look.

"Err, Mila, you have to go home, remember?"

"I know. But I thought . . ."

"We've totally got it figured out," Ashwin said.

"We'll tell you all about it," I said, moving some branches around to hide our armor supplies.

"And you'll get my trike back for real?" Mila tugged at her backpack straps.

"We are definitely getting the trike back," said Ashwin, holding his hands up like she was pointing a water gun at him.

"*Promise* you'll get my trike back for me?" She grabbed her straps tighter.

"Promise," I lied.

I was gonna get it back.

But I was gonna get it back for me.

16.
The Ambush

It was finally time.

Mrs. Vaz let us stay up late to watch a movie, but she went off to bed. We turned the volume way up on the TV. Mrs. Vaz didn't mind—she uses earplugs when she sleeps.

Ashwin snuck into the bathroom and filled up our water guns with his mom's perfume. He wasn't even nervous. "I'll tell her I spilled it."

"She'll believe you," I laughed.

We finished the movie and stuffed ourselves with chips and soda while we waited for Mrs. Vaz's light to go off.

After the little skinny strip of carpet under her bedroom door finally went dark, I could barely sit still. "Let's wait ten more minutes, just to be sure she's asleep," I whispered. Ashwin was all twitchy and excited from the soda too. I wondered again if I should tell him more about Nuts and Buggies, since Mila was finally out of the way. I had been able to convince Ashwin that two skunks stole my trike because it was missing and I stank. But *talking* skunks? I didn't know. The minutes ticked by, and telling him only got harder. What if I was wrong? I hate being wrong. Being wrong is worse than being in trouble.

"Let's go," I finally said.

We snuck out the back door and rummaged around in the bushes for our armor. First off, we ripped apart a bunch of the black trash bags Mila brought. We cut holes for our heads and arms and pulled the bags on. Then we each ripped apart two more bags to cover our arms and legs. I wrapped silver duct tape around the black plastic until it really did look like the plate armor we saw in *Medieval Weapons and Warfare*. I even tore off strips to make a design on our breastplates.

"What is that?" Ashwin asked. "A star?"

"Nah, it's like the spokes of a wheel. You know—for the trike!"

Ashwin wasn't convinced. "Couldn't we have a dragon or something?"

"Sure, Ashwin. Go ahead," I handed him the roll of duct tape. "If you can make a dragon out of duct tape, I'll do all your math homework next week."

"I guess a dragon would be kind of hard. We'll be Knights of the Trike. That's cool, right?"

We nodded and pulled on pairs of goggles, rain boots, and my mom's swimming caps.

"Where should we set up the ambush?" asked Ashwin.

I'd thought about that all day. I knew where we needed to station ourselves, and it wasn't going to be easy.

"By one of Mr. Mendoza's hydrangea hedges," I said. "That's where I found them last night. I think that's where the skunks keep the trike during the day. That's gotta be why Mr. Mendoza thinks we've been messing with his flowers: *trike tracks.*"

"Oh man," groaned Ashwin. "This is not good."

"We don't have a choice. Come on. Let's get our bikes."

My silver Steed shined like a quarter in the moonlight. Ashwin's big sister's old banana-seat, with rusty orange paint, could have been one of Mr. Mendoza's squashed persimmons from last fall.

Ashwin said something really bad under his breath as he yanked his bike out of the ivy. Like, not just impolite. Super bad.

We pushed our rides down the driveway. Our armor made rustling noises and our rain boots kind of clunked against the ground, but we weren't too loud. Ashwin wobbled a little at the sidewalk, when we hopped on the bikes, and then got pedaling fast enough to straighten out. I started slow but soon I zipped into the middle of the street. Riding Steed in the middle of the night is pretty awesome. The cool air and the dark houses and the quiet, empty streets somehow made me feel huge, like something even bigger than a grown-up. Nobody was around. I pedaled harder, and the black trash bag armor flapped around in my super-fast wind.

When Ashwin and I passed by Danny Vega's house, we slowed down a little. I skidded to a stop at his driveway.

"We could do it," I said to Ashwin. "Pop some wheelies in Danny's garden. Pay him back for that soccer ball. We wouldn't even need to go near the trash and Danny's dumb alarm. Nobody would ever know it was us."

I said all that kinda hoping Ashwin wouldn't want to.

'Cause what if we did get caught?

What would happen then?

"Nah," Ashwin said. "It would compromise the real mission. Besides, if anybody did find out it was us, that would mean *definite* war, and this time Johnny would have to back Danny up. I know you still like him. Johnny, I mean. Even though . . ." Ashwin shrugged. He looked away, and I looked away.

Ashwin just gets stuff. Even when you think he's not paying attention, that he might not understand, he is and he does. And he doesn't make a big deal about it.

"Okay!" I grinned. "Let's go set up the ambush."

The two of us crossed to the opposite side of the street and stopped before we got to Mr. Mendoza's house. We stashed our bikes against the wooden fence on the other side of Mr. Mendoza's hedge. Technically we were in Mrs. Pratt's yard, but just being that close to Mr. Mendoza's made me nervous. We crouched down in the dirt next to the fence.

We listened and waited.

I kept my eyes on the sidewalk without blinking.

Even my eyeballs felt excited.

Then we heard them. First a rustling came from the other side of the fence, and then a sharp creak. Ashwin punched my shoulder, and my armor crackled. I held a finger to my lips and then opened my palm up.

Universal kid-code for "shut up and wait."

Then we *really* heard them.

"It's time, Nuts," said a gravelly voice.

"Yes sir, Sergeant Buggies—manning the vehicle!" said the squeaky one, Nuts.

After another rustling sound, I heard something super familiar—a little honk from a horn. The skunks were getting on the trike!

Ashwin's mouth was hanging open. His buckteeth shined in the moonlight. I could tell he had heard them too. So at least I knew I wasn't going nuts. I pointed at the bikes, and he nodded with his eyes bugging out of his head. Maybe I should have told him. But by then it was too late to explain. I pulled my goggles down over my eyes, and so did he.

We hopped on our bikes as quietly as possible. But in black garbage bags, rain boots, and swim goggles, you can't actually do anything quietly.

"Did you hear that, Nuts?"

"I did, sir! Two possible hostile raccoons on our left."

I froze and put my foot on the pedal, ready to push off.

Those skunks were not getting away from me this time.

"Do a quick recon and report back."

A little black-and-white head peeked around the fence and peered into the dark.

"Rotting snail-bait, Sergeant Buggies, I think it's that kid from Caballero Road, and he's got reinforcements."

"You know what to do, Nuts," said the gravelly voice. Buggies.

"Aye-aye, sir! Bringing the stink!" The little skunk whipped around on the sidewalk and did that hand-standy thing again.

But this time I was ready.

"Here it comes, Ashwin. Get ready, and close your mouth!"

The stream of skunk spray came shooting through the moonlight like a falling star. It splattered over our black garbage bags with a sound like a garden hose on a car window.

"I'm hit! I'm hit!" Ashwin said.

I wiped the skunk spray off my goggles.

The little skunk jumped down on all fours again and disappeared into the bushes.

Foopsh!

Both skunks burst out of the blue hydrangea bush, cruising on the trike. They did a quick reversal maneuver and started zooming down the driveway.

"This is it! Let's go!" I yelled to Ashwin. "You go around the corner and head them off. I'll follow them through Mr. Mendoza's yard!"

Ashwin pedaled down the block. His big sister's banana-seat squawked when he went fast. Well, he was going *really* fast—*squawk-squawk-squawk*.

I took a deep breath and peeked into Mr. Mendoza's windows. There was a blue light, like a TV left on, but no Mendoza. I pushed off hard and raced down the driveway after the skunks.

I could see the skunks pedaling up-down-up-down. They were rolling along the gravel path through Mr. Mendoza's orchard.

I ducked under a low, bare branch on the orchard's apple tree. Then I coasted around the curve in the yard's path, spraying gravel behind Steed.

I saw Ashwin skid to a stop on the sidewalk ahead. His bike blocked off the end of the path. We were totally going to get them. The skunks did another reversal on the trike and turned around, but they could see me coming fast.

I parked Steed across my end of the path, blocking their way.

"There's nowhere to go," I panted. "Give up the trike." I pulled out my water gun.

"Yeah, hand it over," Ashwin said, pulling his water pistol out too.

The two skunks looked at each other over the handlebars of the trike. I swear the big one started to laugh at us.

"Oh, noooooo," Buggies said. "They've got *water* guns—better run for it."

"All right, Caballero," Nuts said in a squeaky little voice. "You asked for it."

The skunks turned the trike around and grabbed the handlebars tight. They were going to ram straight into Ashwin!

"Uh-oh," Ashwin said.

17.
The Skirmish

We both started squirting perfume at the skunks like crazy, but that didn't do much. Ashwin even got the little one in the face, which had to sting. Nuts squeezed his eyes shut and kept pedaling while Buggies steered.

"Prepare for impact, Nuts!" said Buggies.

"Ready as rotting snail-bait, sir!"

The two skunks picked up a lot of speed. They hunkered down and held on tight, ready for the crash that was coming.

Ashwin's eyes bugged out under his skunk-spray-protection goggles, and he tried to pedal out of the way. He wobbled a little and was about to make it when . . .

Chhhhunk!

The trike crashed right into the rusty wheel of Ashwin's bike. He went down. Really hard. The trike tipped up onto two wheels, but both skunks leaned in and clunked it back down onto the sidewalk. And they just kept pedaling.

The skunks were getting away *again*!

Our weapons were useless. My support was trapped under a heap of orange bicycle, and I didn't know what to do next. I threw my water gun down and pedaled after the skunks quick as I could. My black trash bag armor flapped in the air.

The skunks were barely to the next driveway when I caught up to them on Steed. I swerved in front of the trike, and we crashed in a tangle of wheels and handlebars. My bike toppled to the ground. I ripped a new hole in my red sweats, skinning my knee. My old trike was tipped on its side. The skunks had been knocked off like two little bowling pins.

I did it!

I totally did it!

I got them.

I was laying there under my bike, with my skinned knee oozing blood, as Nuts and Buggies hopped up, shook themselves off, and pushed the trike back onto its wheels. Before I had time to blink, they climbed onto the pedals and grabbed the handlebars.

"See you around, Caballero," said Nuts.

They were gonna get away.

Again.

Then, in this shivery rustle of branches and blossoms, something exploded out of the hedge next to the sidewalk. It was Mila, in a boots-off-the-ground leap, wearing my old fireman costume. She held her pink butterfly net high over her shoulder.

Bam! Her black boots cracked down on the sidewalk.

"Not so fast, you stinkers," she said. "That's *my* trike."

Mila smacked the butterfly net down and scooped up Nuts. She swung him through the air and smacked the net down again and scooped up Buggies. He was way too big for her to swing, though, so after Mila slammed the open end of the butterfly net down on the sidewalk, she stood on the handle in her black cowgirl boots.

I . . . I could not believe it. Sometimes when Mila wakes me up early in the morning and she's got her peacock fluff of hair all puffed up in back, I can't help but smile and be glad to see her—you know, before I really wake up and remember that she's my little sister and she bugs me. Seeing her jump out of those bushes and swoop up the skunks in her pink net was kind of like waking up. I couldn't help it. I smiled.

Ashwin came running up behind me and helped lift Steed off my leg.

I stayed sprawled on the concrete, smiling at Mila like a goofus.

"Don't just sit there, Mateo," Mila said. "Help me keep these stinkers trapped."

Nuts and Buggies were both struggling under the net. Mila wobbled and caught her balance every time the skunks wiggled. Pretty soon they were gonna knock her down too.

I pushed myself up from the concrete with my elbow

and hopped over on one foot, 'cause my knee was still stinging. I stood on the handle of the butterfly net while Mila and Ashwin got down on all fours and held down the net's edges. Ashwin put his face close, pushing his goggles up to get a better look at Nuts and Buggies.

"Careful," I told him. "You never know when those things are gonna blow."

"Right," said Ashwin, sliding the goggles back down. He put his face right up against the net again. "So, do they really . . . really, um . . . ?"

"Talk?" I said.

"Yeah . . . talk," Ashwin said, giving the little one a tiny poke through the net.

"That's right, Canela," said Nuts. "We talk."

Ashwin jumped up. "Whoa," he said, backing away. "That little mutant knows I live on Calle Canela, Mateo. This is so not cool."

Buggies rammed his snout at the edge of the net, trying to lift it up as soon as Ashwin let go.

"Quick, Canela," Mila said. "Don't let them get away."

"Hey," Ashwin said, grabbing the net. "Whose side are you on?"

"Mine," said Mila, glaring at me. "You stinkers left me out, and Mateo was keeping secrets!"

Mila and Ashwin both glared at me. Hard. "I . . . I, uh . . . well, I wasn't *sure*. I thought maybe I was going a little crazy, or, you know . . . I could have been wrong."

"Whoa, Mateo. How scary for you," Ashwin said.

As Buggies started bashing at the net again, Ashwin asked, "What are we going to do with these guys?"

"Yeah, what are you gonna do with us, Caballero?" squeaked Nuts.

"Quiet, Nuts. We're in enemy hands."

"Yes sir, Sergeant Buggies. Going quiet." Nuts crossed his little skunk arms.

Mila peered into the net. "They do have names!" she said.

"Yeah, the little squeaky one is Nuts, and the big one is Buggies," I told them.

"What do you want with my trike, you stinkers?" Mila was only inches away from both skunk butts.

"From what I hear, it ain't your trike, Polka Dots," Buggies said in his gravelly voice.

"Hey, sir—quiet, right?"

"The mission is a wash anyway, Nuts. We wouldn't make it tonight, even if we weren't prisoners of war." Both skunks stared up the hill toward our school.

"Make it where?" me and Ashwin asked at the same time.

The skunks squinted at each other. Buggies nodded to Nuts. "The playground. The raccoons always stake it out, but they don't even head up there until they see us coming. They just don't want *us* to use it. And once the raccoon army establishes a secure position atop the play structure, they start launching missiles at us."

"Our enemy is bigger and faster. We need the trike

so we can outmaneuver them and make it up there first," Buggies grunted.

"What's so important about the school playground?" I asked.

"Slides. We really like the slides," said Buggies.

"We ain't about to let those chubby trash-eaters push us around, either," said Nuts.

I could tell me and Ashwin were thinking the same thing. "Danny Vega," Ashwin said, crossing his arms.

I nodded.

Ashwin leaned down real close to the skunks. He poked at Nuts with his shoe. "Helping these guys sounds like it *could* be a righteous mission, Mateo. This could be our chance to finally have some fun."

"What? You want to ride up to the playground with these guys? You're the one who called them mutants."

Ashwin took another long look at the skunks. "Yeah . . . but wouldn't that be cool? Riding our bikes all over school at night?"

"Maybe . . ." I nodded slowly, trying to figure everything out. Trying to decide. Helping the skunks on their mission sounded like it *could* be pretty cool. Those raccoons were like Danny and Martin, taking over the playground for no reason I could understand. I couldn't do anything about Danny Vega taking Johnny away, anything about them kicking balls at us up on the monkey bars, but this was different. We could totally take back the playground. At night, it could be all ours.

A place where honor would rule. Maybe this was our chance. But then I remembered about the Vegas' garage and the missing stuff and all the trash. "It could be a righteous mission," I said. "Or it could be a trick."

I stared down at the two skunks stuck in Mila's net. Buggies sat on his butt, with his little skunk belly pouching over his feet. Nuts glared at me with his tiny arms crossed. And Mila was staring at me too. Like she trusted me.

But I wasn't sure what I wanted to do.

I wasn't sure what I was *supposed* to do.

"Sir, raccoons at twelve o'clock," squeaked Nuts.

We checked the sidewalk. A few blocks away, a group of raccoons scrambled down the street. When the raccoons crossed under the streetlights, all their eyes glinted like a bag of red marbles. They made gross trilling noises when they walked. A big one up front kept turning around and snarling at the others to keep them in line.

"The raccoons don't talk," Ashwin said. "They just make gross animal sounds."

"'Course they don't talk," Buggies said. "They're raccoons."

Ashwin gave me this bug-eyed look, but I still wasn't sure about what to do.

The smaller raccoons followed the big one up a driveway. They knocked down a set of garbage cans near someone's grass. In barely a minute, the whole lawn was covered with trash.

"Why do they do that?" I asked. "Are they looking for food?"

"Negative, Caballero," said Nuts.

"Raccoons are trash-eaters, true," Buggies said. "But mostly they do it because they can."

Nuts and Buggies twitched in the net, watching the raccoons make their gross mess. The skunks seemed pretty small with their fur all squashed down, and the raccoons looked huge lumbering across that lawn. Dangerous, even—from far away, I could feel it. I guess they got bored with scattering the trash. The biggest one snarled, and they all moved on down the sidewalk.

Toward us.

The raccoons were only a block and a half away.

And they were getting louder.

"Holy monkeys, Mateo! Don't raccoons spread rabies or something?" asked Ashwin.

"I . . . I think so," I said. "But only if they already have it. And only if they bite you."

"Jeez, man. I think those things might have it—don't you?"

The skunks started to wriggle really hard—they were kinda freaking out—and Mila stepped closer to me. She grabbed onto my hand, and I let her hold it.

"We've got to get them to take us to Stink Base, sir. We're in an insecure position, and I think the raccoons have spotted us," Nuts said.

I kept checking on the skunks and then the

raccoons. Skunks. Raccoons. Skunks. And the next time I looked at the raccoons, the big one stood up on his back feet and snarled. I took a half step back without really meaning to.

Buggies heaved up off his butt, leaned as close as he could to me. "Let us out, kid. Let us out and run for it. An enemy this vicious so close at hand calls for a full retreat. There is no loss of honor in protecting your weaponry. We've got to get the trike back to Stink Base."

Down the sidewalk, the biggest raccoon started loping a little faster, and the other raccoons came bumping after him. Mila let go of my hand, hopped onto the seat of the trike, and grabbed the handlebars.

"Don't let them get it, Mateo!" she said.

She backpedaled a little toward me, and the empty bucket of the trike bumped the handle of the net. That's when I decided what to do. I swooped the net up with both skunks inside, then slammed it down on the trike bucket. The skunks were still trapped under the netting, but we would be able to move them. Well, almost trapped.

"Ashwin, duct tape!"

Ashwin lunged over and pulled a half-used roll of tape out of the basket on the front of his bike. I held the rim of the net against the trike bucket while Ashwin duct-taped it on.

"I'm not letting you out. Not yet. You guys are coming with us."

Every time Ashwin ripped off a new piece of duct tape, I flinched a little. *Schrrrr. Snap.* A couple more pieces and the net would be secure. The skunks really would be our prisoners of war.

"Hurry up, Canela," Mila shouted at Ashwin. "They're almost here."

The raccoons loomed out of the dark. Half a block away. I could only see their sloped backs, but I could actually hear their claws clicking on the concrete. Once the raccoons got to the next streetlight, we were going to be dead—maybe rabies-infested—meat.

After Ashwin put one more piece of tape on the net, I shoved him over toward his bike. "Mount up!" I said. "Nuts, Buggies, take us to your base."

Nuts leaned in to murmur in Buggies' ear. He sounded like a creaky wheel. I only heard the words *supplies* and *borrow* before Buggies gave a little nod.

"All right," said Buggies. "Let's RTB, but we have to travel in tight formation. We can't have those trash-eaters see us going in."

"Or we'll be snail-bait for sure," squeaked Nuts.

"What's *RTB*?" asked Mila, her eyeballs getting all shiny.

I just shrugged.

Ashwin tipped his rusty bike up off the ground. "Don't worry, Polka Dots," he told Mila, "it just means 'Return to Base.'"

"How did you know that?" I asked.

"I don't know," he shrugged. "Maybe from a movie?"

I climbed up onto Steed. "Tell Mila where to go. We'll follow you guys." Mila looked up at me. She seemed kinda scared but started rolling when Nuts whispered squeaky directions in her ear. I pedaled after them.

We all rode off in a tight triangle formation—Mila leading the way, me and Ashwin coming behind—watching each flank for red-eyed raccoons. When we got to the corner, Mila made a hard left and I checked over my shoulder. The raccoons were rumbling along under the streetlight, sniffing at the roll of duct tape we had left on the sidewalk. I turned the corner and didn't peek back again. Our armor crackled, but otherwise we stayed pretty quiet. I listened for the click of claws behind us for a couple blocks, but I guess we lost them. I took a few deep breaths but I could still feel my heart beating in the tips of my ears.

Then all of a sudden, we were *there*.

"Welcome to Stink Base," Buggies said.

18.
The Base

So, I can't really tell you where Stink Base is. I promised I wouldn't. It's kind of on the way home, kind of not. As we rode there, Nuts and Buggies were still trapped in the bucket of the trike, their black-and-white fur pressed against the pink mesh net.

"Let us out, Caballero, before the raccoons track our position," said Nuts.

When I caught Ashwin's eye, I could tell he was a little disappointed, and I was too. I'd imagined their base would be awesome. I mean, they were skunks that stole stuff, talked, and could ride a trike.

But Stink Base was only a big hedge.

I could have walked right past it.

I *had* walked right past it, maybe a million times.

"What you waiting for?" said Buggies. "Let us out so we can move this operation to a secure location."

I wasn't 100 percent sure about setting them free. I just had to go with my gut.

I pried the net off the trike's bucket. The trike tipped a little with Mila in it, but she didn't say anything. Both skunks leaped out of the bucket, shook their fur, and stood back to back, checking their surroundings with their paws up. For a second, I thought we were in for it.

Another attack.

But after scanning the street, Buggies said, "No enemies sighted. Lead us in, Nuts."

"Yes sir, Sergeant Buggies!" Nuts bent down and fumbled under the edge of the bush. He grabbed hold of an old white rope and started to tug. I heard the screechy whine of a pulley, and the front of the hedge lifted away like a garage door.

We all went inside. I mean, like, *deep* inside the hedge. Me and Ashwin left our bikes on the sidewalk, but Mila rode the trike right into Stink Base. There was a ramp dug into the ground—an entrance tunnel. Old black and white linoleum tiles lined the floor and the walls. It was exactly like the tile we used to have in our kitchen before Dad put the wood in last year. The skunks' feet clicked against the linoleum as they disappeared down the ramp and off into some kind of room. It was way dark, but Mila rolled right after them.

After more skittering of skunk feet on the tiles, some lights turned on.

Christmas twinkle lights were hanging down from the ceiling. Me and Ashwin had to duck so we wouldn't knock them down. Stink Base is pretty big—I mean, if you're a skunk. The room curved like the bottom of an empty pool. The skunks had propped up scavenged tarps with ropes and old broom handles to make a ceiling. We could see bits of the thick hedge peeking through under the tarps. And I spotted two tiny bunks carved into the wall, half covered with dishrag curtains. Mila hopped off the trike and tried to curl up in one but even she was too big.

"Get your big feet out of my bunk, Polka Dots," squeaked Nuts.

Above the black and white tiles, there were shelves dug into the room's dirt walls. Cool stuff covered every part of them. Old pickle jars filled with food, stray screws, bent nails, power tools, old garden hoses, and extension cords.

"Nice," I said, nodding. "These are some righteous raw materials."

"Welcome to Military Appropriations," said Buggies, waving at the shelves.

Nuts unscrewed the top of a glass jar and started crunching something. He tossed a few to Buggies.

"Any of the chocolate-covered grasshopper rations left?" asked Buggies.

"Nah. We've only got almonds—sorry, sir," said Nuts.

"Ah, nuts!" Buggies shrugged and started to munch away.

"Help yourselves, stinkers," said Nuts, offering the open jar.

I was the only one who took an almond. I could see a couple of moldy ones near the bottom, and all the chocolate had gone white and crusty like Halloween candy that's been in your room too long. But it was totally okay.

Crunch.

Crunch.

Crunch.

We were safe, and I had the trike (kinda), but I still had a bunch of questions. I wasn't sure what to do or where to sit. There were only two tiny lawn chairs, the kind for toddlers, set up next to a tree stump table. I stood in the middle of the room, bending over a little so my head wouldn't bump into the lights.

Ashwin started poking around in the shelves. Mila took down a skateboard with three wheels and sat on it, trying to ride down the slope of the tiled floor.

"Where did you get all this stuff?" asked Ashwin.

Nuts chewed on a chocolate-covered almond, really loud, like "this is the only answer you're gonna get," and Buggies crossed his arms.

"I think I might know," I said. "Remember what I told you about the Vega house?" I turned to Buggies and Nuts. "You guys have been stealing stuff from all over the neighborhood. Mom and Dad think it's *me.*"

Nuts just shrugged and crunched another almond. "Like I said, welcome to Military Appropriations. These supplies were taken in name of the Midnight War. Show 'em your scar, Nuts."

Nuts pushed back the fur on one side of his head. That's when I noticed that he pretty much only had one ear. "Tore it right off," squeaked Nuts. He flopped down into one of the little chairs.

"Oh, jeez!" said Ashwin. "Mateo, these guys probably have rabies too. That's it! That's gotta be it!" He started back up the ramp, but Mila was squinting at me with her head cocked. I could tell she wanted me to decide whether the skunks were okay or not.

Well, the skunks had definitely stolen all their supplies, and some of that Mom and Dad blamed on *me*. But Stink Base *was* pretty cool, and I could see the skunks were at war. They needed a base. Somewhere they could be safe. I guess "Military Appropriations" was their only choice. I mean, skunks can't just go to the hardware store and buy stuff. So I decided to be okay with it as long as I didn't keep getting the blame. And, yeah, there was definitely, absolutely, something weird about Nuts and Buggies, but I didn't think they were rabid.

"Hold up, man," I said to Ashwin before he disappeared up the tunnel. "I don't think these guys have rabies. But I don't know about those raccoons."

"Negative and negative, sir," said Buggies. "We are clear of that particular virus, and as far as we know, so are the raccoons."

"So . . . how did you guys get this way?" I asked.

"Yeah, and why don't the raccoons talk too?" asked Ashwin, creeping back from the tunnel one step at a time.

I waited for an answer, but Buggies just shifted on his paws. I swear I heard a couple of crickets chirp. Nuts crossed his little skunk arms like Mila does when she doesn't want to tell Mom something. He stared me dead in the face without blinking. No answer.

Buggies sniffed a little. "Nuts, I think they deserve to know . . . But Caballero, we just don't have any answers."

"What do you mean? You guys have to know!"

Nuts squinted sideways at Buggies, and they both shrugged together.

"Every once in a while Nuts gets a wild idea . . . ," Buggies said, "but that's all we've got. Good guesswork."

"Like the commander said—" Nuts pointed at me with one of his tiny claws. "—some things just don't have any explanation, Caballero. No matter how much you want them to."

"Cooooool!" said Ashwin, nodding his head real slow.

I could tell Ashwin was already thinking up a hundred different explanations for the skunks. Like maybe they were some experiment gone wrong, maybe they were some alien hybrid, or maybe they were just magic. I think as long as he knew he could never figure it out, he was okay dreaming about all those maybes. But I . . . I wanted a reason.

"Nothing about this is cool," I said. "There has to be an explanation. You guys came from *somewhere*. And what about those raccoons?"

Both skunks kinda rolled their eyes, like, "we don't

have to explain anything to you, " and I guess they didn't. They were right in front of me, and I was pretty sure they weren't holding anything back. I'm not saying I didn't want to know where they came from. I did. I still do. But wherever they did come from, they were *real*.

"Okay." I put my hands up. "We can't let those raccoons trash the neighborhood and take over the playground every night. These guys need our help, so we need a plan."

"Yeah," said Mila. "Ms. Printz says throwing stuff is *not* allowed and we have to share the playground at school with *everyone*."

"We tried that, Polka Dots. No dice," said Nuts.

"Sharing is *not* an option. Does Nuts have to show you his scar again?" asked Buggies.

Mila glared at both skunks.

"Somebody should be riding those slides all the time," Ashwin said, coming closer. "Even at night. You're right, Mateo. It's a righteous mission. I can feel it!"

I could feel it too. So I went with what I believed was right. Those skunks were a little weird, but I think all they wanted was to have some fun in a place that was really theirs. Just like me and Ashwin.

"All right," I said. "Me and Ashwin are the Knights of the Trike, and we've got a proposal for you. How 'bout we join ranks? You guys could . . . be in charge of appropriations."

Mila scrunched her mouth up. She had been asking

me for months to be a knight, but little sisters *can't* be knights—you have to be a squire first—and I thought she was way too little even to be a squire. Anyway, we didn't have time to argue about that.

"Negative," growled Buggies, crossing his paws.

"Sergeant Buggies is the OIC here," squeaked Nuts.

"Oick? What's an oick?" I asked, totally confused.

Buggies put his paws on his head like Mom sometimes does at the end of the day.

Ashwin leaned in. "I think they mean *O-I-C*, like Officer in Charge."

"Oh. Well, that's cool with us, right, Ashwin?"

"Right! Sure," he said. "You guys could have, um . . . tactical command."

Buggies kept rubbing his head. "None of these guys even have security clearance," he mumbled. Nuts leaned in to squeak-whisper in Buggies's ear, but all I caught was the word *trike*.

"We accept your proposed alliance, sir," said both skunks, coming to attention.

"I can promote you both to technical sergeants, which will give you the appropriate clearance," Buggies continued, "but Nuts and I must maintain tactical command."

"We take turns," squeaked Nuts. "Sergeant Buggies is your OIC until he's relieved of duty after the midnight mission. Is that clear, sirs?"

Me and Ashwin grinned. "Yes, sir," we both said, saluting.

"What do you mean, you take turns?" Mila asked. But nobody had time to answer.

An alarm went off. Like the kind that wakes you up in the morning:

Beep. Beep. Beep.

Beep. Beep. Beep.

Beep. Beep. Beep.

"The perimeter alarm has been triggered, sir. Possible raccoon a block from the main entrance," whispered Nuts.

Ashwin shoved my arm. "Holy monkeys, man. Your new bike is up there."

"Quiet, Sergeant Canela," squeaked Nuts.

We all listened as that gross raccoon trilling came out of a baby monitor on one of the shelves.

Mila ran over to the trike, jammed herself into the seat, and pedaled forward, back, forward, back, covering the tiles again and again, watching my face the whole time. I guess she was waiting to see what I would do.

"The raccoons are a block away, on the north side of the entrance," whispered Nuts.

"They'll sight the bikes any second," said Buggies, pacing over the black and white tiles. "There's no reason for those vehicles to be out on the sidewalk at night. The raccoons are sure to do a little recon, and if they start nosing around up there, our position won't be secure. Stink Base could be compromised."

"We've got to move the bikes, Sergeant Buggies," I said. "We've still got time to keep Stink Base a secret.

And we could still win the Midnight War. Let's get up there, mount up, and stake out our position on top of the playground!"

"He's right, Sergeant Buggies," said Nuts.

"Agreed." Buggies said. "Stage one of our mission will be moving those bikes away from Stink Base. We've got to be mounted and en route before the raccoons spot us. Stage two will be taking the school playground."

Me, Ashwin, and Nuts all nodded. Mila just gripped the handles of the trike harder and looked, I don't know, determined.

"All right, soldiers—it's go time." Buggies held up his fist, counting on his clawed fingers. "Let's move out on three."

Then he mouthed:

One.

Two.

Three!

19.
The Midnight War

On *three*, me and Ashwin charged up the ramp, ready to mount our bikes and move them away from the entrance of Stink Base—stage one of the Midnight War offensive. I didn't even want to think about having that cool hideout raided by raccoons because of *us*.

Nuts and Buggies hopped into the back bucket of the trike.

"Move 'em out, Polka Dots," squeaked Nuts.

But Mila didn't pedal up the ramp. She just grabbed those handlebars tight and scrunched her face up. "No way, Mateo. Not on my trike!"

Ashwin skidded to a stop halfway up the ramp. He bugged his eyes out at me. "Mateo, let's go." He totally got it, as usual. Ashwin understands stuff like honor, duty, and the price of being beaten by someone bigger. Stuff I didn't think Mila could understand. But I had to try to convince her anyway.

"Come on, Mila," I said. "This is our only chance.

This is a Midnight War for playground freedom. Those marble-eyed monsters are the ones who've been trashing our neighborhood. The skunks just want to have some fun. Don't you want to help?"

"No*pe*," she said, smacking her *p*. "Actually, maybe. But nobody asked *me* to be a knight."

We did *not* have time for this.

I motioned for Ashwin. When he ran over I whispered in his ear, then we both grabbed onto the back of the trike and pushed Mila up the ramp, skunks and all.

"We can't push her all the way to the playground, Mateo," Ashwin wheezed. "We'll never beat the raccoons if we don't ride our bikes."

"Just get her to the sidewalk," I panted. "I have an idea."

We popped out of the bush in a little explosion of leaves, and Nuts secured the swinging door behind us. I couldn't see the raccoons yet, but I knew they were out there in the dark. Somewhere.

"Ashwin, grab our bikes and move them away from the entrance of Stink Base." I pushed Mila down the sidewalk, as far from the entrance as I could. Ashwin rolled our bikes over one at a time. We ended up in a dark patch of pavement between two streetlights. In our black-trash-bag-duct-taped-skunk-proof armor, I felt almost invisible.

I checked up the north side of the block again, and there they were. The raccoons. We could barely see their humped shapes, but even that far away, the danger of them all hit me like a nightmare. But I wasn't sleeping, and I wasn't alone.

"Look, Mila," I said. "You've gotta come with us. Otherwise those raccoons will get you *and* the trike."

"No*pe*," she said again. "I decided. I'm taking the trike home. It's closer than school anyway."

Nuts hopped impatiently, and Buggies shook his head like he couldn't believe he'd gone to war with a bunch of amateurs. The raccoons rambled closer, but I didn't think they had spotted us yet.

"Please, Mila," I said. "The skunks need the trike. We've got to help them take the playground."

"If I help, what do I get?" asked Mila, crossing her arms.

"Cinnamon buns," Ashwin whispered. "You can come over whenever my mom makes them."

"Not good enough. What else?"

"We can play tic-tac-toe every day," I said. "And I'll let you win. And you can be our squire—almost like you're a Knight of the Trike, but in training."

She scrinched her eyes at me. "No way. I caught the skunks. I want to be a *real* knight."

"Fine. You're a full knight, Sir Peacock Head."

"And I like my code name better. Polka Dots."

"All *right*, you're Polka Dots. Now let's *go*. What else could you possibly want?"

"You knowwwww . . . ," said Mila.

I could see the raccoons over the top of Mila's head. They were coming straight for us. Their shapes became clearer, but I still couldn't spot the glint of their eyes. At least we'd accomplished stage one of our mission—we were far enough away to keep Stink Base secret. But what about stage two? We needed the trike, and for that, we needed Mila.

I knew what she wanted.

I had known it the whole time.

"I'll give it to you," I said.

"For keeps? You'll stop calling it your trike?"

I thought about the raccoons getting closer, and Ashwin all excited and ready to roll on his crummy bike, and the two weird skunks in Mila's back bucket.

"Yep," I said. "For keeps."

"Okay," she said. "Let's ride!"

"Yes sir, Polka Dots," said Nuts.

"Move 'em out!" said Buggies.

I pushed Steed up onto its wheels. Ashwin creaked onto his rusty old tank of a bike. Then Mila started pedaling. Nuts leaned out of the bucket, snatched Mila's pink butterfly net off the ground, and held it high in the air like a standard. We rode down one of those little curb ramp things and out into the middle of the street. Me and Ashwin on the outside, Mila and the skunks in between. We didn't even use the crosswalk.

Mila pedaled hard to keep up.

I glanced back, swerving a little on my bike. When

I saw the raccoons, I almost lost my balance. Almost. "They spotted us," I said. The big one stood up on its back feet, snarling. All the other raccoons bumped up behind it, staring down the sidewalk. They turned into Mr. Mendoza's driveway and loped away in a heap of dark shadows.

"They're cutting through Geezer's Garden," Buggies groaned. "The shortcut will spit them out straight over by the park. Then all they need to do to take the school playground is sneak up the hill!"

"Pedals to the metal!" squeaked Nuts.

We raced toward the corner, still in the middle of the street. Still in triangle formation. I pushed as hard as I could, ignoring the sting of my skinned knee, until my legs got achy under my armor and sweats. The hedges and houses were dark and blurry as we rolled past.

By the time we turned the corner, those raccoons had already made it across the street. They were disappearing into Oak Park. I knew where they were headed.

"They're cutting across the creek," I panted.

"Affirmative, Sergeant Caballero. But we've got to keep to the streets if we have any chance of over-taking them."

"I know. But . . . can you do it, Mila? Can you make it up the hill and keep up?" I wasn't so sure.

Mila pedaled faster. "Told you, Caballero—I can carry anything."

The skunks hunkered down in the trike's bucket like little jockeys, their fur flickering in the wind. We cut around Oak Park and pedaled up the hill. Mila was practically purple, she was pushing those pedals so hard. But she made it. When we got to Las Positas, I could see the school. I even got a little peek of the playground through the fence. We were gonna do it. Then I saw the little red hand blinking at the crosswalk, and I remembered my promise to Mom.

"Geezer farts," I said.

I cut out in front of Mila and Ashwin—*screeeech*—and braked.

Mila banged right into Steed.

"Hang on," I panted. "We've got to dismount."

"What do you mean, dismount? They're going to beat us!" Mila was maybe madder than I'd ever seen her.

I punched the metal button.

"I promised Mom we would use the crosswalk."

"Ah, jeez, Mateo. It's the middle of the night. It doesn't count!" Ashwin groaned.

"Caballero, this is totally nuts," squeaked Nuts.

Mila bumped into Steed, just nosing out, *clink-clink*, pestering me to get going. "Come on, Caballero. I'm a full knight now! I should be able to cross the street just like you. Mom's rules don't count at night."

I didn't budge. "You're still my little sister, even in the middle of the night. Even though you're a full knight. And promises always count—I know that much."

I knew we were losing our lead. My heart thumped like a countdown clock.

"Raccoons at nine o'clock," said Buggies.

I scanned Las Positas up and down. There were no cars. I couldn't even hear any traffic down on the freeway. But I saw the raccoons burst out of this dark alley between two houses, straight onto the huge four-lane road. They crept across like oil stains and made it to the other side before the red hand at the crosswalk stopped blinking. They started loping up the driveway and through the school parking lot.

The creepy electronic voice counted down: *ten . . . nine . . . eight . . .*

The white walking guy was blinking.

"Charge!" I shouted, pushing my bike across the street.

Mila pedaled next to me, refusing to get off the trike. Her pink butterfly net drooped in Nuts's paws. Ashwin pushed his bike next to me. "Can't believe you're making us do this, man."

We made it to other side right when the raccoons disappeared into the dark of the school grounds. I mounted Steed. Ashwin hopped on his rusty bike with a *squawk*, and we all pedaled after those raccoons.

Being at school in the middle of the night makes your heart beat faster than riding your bike uphill. The sound of our spinning wheels echoed off the long outdoor hallways. *Whup-whup-click-click-click.* Then, out on the blacktop of the basketball courts, that weird echo disappeared.

The raccoons scrambled down the path to the play-ground while we were still at the edge of the field. We whizzed past the metal lunch tables, cut across the lumpy grass, and bumped onto the asphalt path behind the rac-coons. They were within striking distance of the play structure, maybe thirty feet away. We only had a few seconds to close the gap.

"We'll have to go straight through them," I shouted. We pedaled up with our armor rustling in the wind. I took the left. Ashwin took the right. We both skidded to a stop in front of the raccoons, blocking the path. They tumbled into a heap and turned around.

And there was Mila.

She pedaled right into the middle of them, and Nuts flung Mila's butterfly net like a spear. Then he and Buggies hopped out of the back bucket and did their handstand thing. Next to the raccoons, the skunks looked even littler than before, but they squared off and let their stink fly. The big raccoon out front got hit with both streams of gooey spray.

The whole enemy army scattered like bowling pins. Me and Ashwin threw our bikes down on the trampled grass at the edge of the field and ran for it. The skunks were right behind us. Ashwin scaled the wooden ladder closest to the field, and then so did I.

Some kids had made a pile of pinecones at the top of the big metal slide under the west tower. Me and Ash-win each picked up two of those spiky seed fortresses and checked the field of battle. The pinecones were heavy and pricked at my skin. They smelled like sap and dust. The two of us chucked them at the raccoons. After a few shots, most of the enemy army ran to hide behind the trunks of the big trees. I got at least three raccoons, but I don't think Ashwin got any. Every time my hits connected, I heard the raccoons *skrarg-skrarg-skrarg*ing in the dark. A few raccoons were already retreating across the blacktop and back toward the school buildings.

The skunks skittered up the metal slide and did a little victory dance next to us. Ashwin started dancing too—he made me laugh—but I didn't dance.

Not yet.

Mila was still down on the path, scattering the rest of the raccoons. The big one was rubbing at its eyes, hunched in the same spot on the path where it got sprayed. It snarled, grunted, and rubbed its fuzzy face again.

The raccoon opened its eyes one at a time.

I could see them glinting in the night.

So I knew it could see.

That big raccoon lumbered right over to my shiny new bike, Steed. The raccoon sniffed and nibbled at the seat. It even tried to lift the bike a little, fiddling with the kickstand, but I didn't think it was strong enough to get Steed up alone, and the other raccoons were running off into the night.

Mila came speeding up toward Steed. "Back off,

you trash-eater," she shouted.

The lead raccoon's fur stuck up in pokey cowlicks. It had to smell really bad.

The smell of a skunk can deter a dangerous predator. I read that in the library book from school.

But could that smell stop Mila Augustina Martinez?

No*pe.*

She rushed toward the big stinky raccoon, and it backed away from my bike. The raccoon stood up on its back paws.

Every time Mila creaked past, the raccoon backed off, and every time she rolled away, the raccoon came slinking over to my bike again. It kept lifting Steed a little higher, and then, *sprong*, it got my kickstand down. The bike was balanced on two wheels, ready to be mounted. As he—or I guess it could've been a she—clicked its mouth, the other raccoons came sneaking back out from behind the tree trunks. They darted across the school field, toward Mila and Steed. Me and Ashwin chucked more pinecones, but we were running out. Also, Ashwin doesn't have the best aim.

The big raccoon clambered up Steed and actually put its chubby butt on the seat. Mila kept charging on the trike, but the big raccoon wasn't backing off anymore. It was trying to reach for my handlebars, still clicking at its buddies while they circled up behind Mila.

Mila couldn't see the others rushing in behind her,

and she couldn't know we were almost out of ammo.

"Come on, Polka Dots, get your butt up here," I shouted.

Mila's face looked woke-up-from-a-nightmare scared when she saw all those raccoons coming for her. But she gripped the handles of her trike and started zooming at the whole circle of them.

"No way, Mateo. They're gonna get your new bike!" Mila yelled.

Nuts and Buggies shrugged.

"Too bad, Caballero. It's a fierce piece of machinery," Nuts said.

"The cost of victory," Buggies added sadly.

Ashwin picked up the last two pinecones and got ready to chuck them out. "What's our next move?" he asked.

For a second, I didn't know. I didn't want to go down there with that marble-eyed monster on the loose, but I definitely didn't want to lose Steed.

Then I heard Mila shriek, "Ahhhhh! Ahhhh! Ahhh!"

One of the littler raccoons had hopped in her bucket and started yanking at her back. It was trying to clamber up higher. I could hear the strange sound of claws on Mila's plastic fireman costume. The raccoon *skrarg-skarg-skrarg*ed at her, lunging for her neck.

"Ahhhh! Mateooooo!"

I snatched the last two pinecones from Ashwin and thumped down the slide. *Boom-boom-squeeee . . .* the metal hissed under my sneakers. When I was close enough for a good shot, I took aim and let the pinecone fly.

Thunk!

I got the little raccoon in the back of the head. It tumbled off Mila, stood up, shook its face, and ran off into the night. Mila didn't stop for a second. She kept racing around in a tight circle, scattering raccoons away from my bike—"Ahhhhhhhhhhhhhh!"

Only the biggest raccoon was still close enough to attack Mila.

It hopped down from Steed and reared up, ready to lunge at her.

I squeezed the last pinecone in my hand, watching the gross, growling raccoon.

I pulled my arm back, whispered a swear, and let it fly.

Ka-chuuunk!

I got it. Right between the eyes.

The big raccoon fell down on the asphalt path.

His claws grabbed at the air a little.

Ashwin and the skunks whooped behind me on the playground tower. The rest of the raccoons skittered across the blacktop basketball courts, down the open school hallway, and then disappeared across the street.

"Whoa! Did you kill it?" asked Mila, pedaling up next to me. She was breathing hard and pretending not to be totally freaked out.

We bent down over the raccoon. It did kind of look

dead, but it also looked like it could eat our faces off if it woke up.

"I don't know." I started gathering extra ammo off the ground and tossing it into Mila's bucket. You know—in case it wasn't dead.

Thump. Thump. Thump.

The raccoon twitched, and Mila and I jerked back, and maybe I shrieked a little.

I grabbed Steed, and me and Mila raced toward the playground tower, stopping to toss more pine-cones in Mila's bucket along the way. She parked at the bottom of the slide, and I slid the pinecones up one at a time.

Ashwin, Nuts, and Buggies caught them and stacked them all into another pile at the top of the slide.

"Quick, Mateo! It's getting up," said Mila.

I stashed Steed as far under the playground structure as I could, then shoved Mila's trike under too.

"Come on—come on!" shouted Mila, bouncing up and down on the bottom of the slide.

We thumped up together, grabbing the cold metal bar at the top.

When I turned, I saw the big raccoon lurching forward again. The red eyes glared at us. Ashwin's persimmon-colored banana-seat bike was just lying there, waiting to be snatched.

"Sorry, man. We couldn't get yours too." I shook my head.

"That's okay. Do you think they'll take it?" asked Ashwin, kinda hopeful.

"Negative, looks like the raccoons are in full retreat, Sergeant Canela," Nuts said.

"Oh, well," said Ashwin, picking up a pinecone but not chucking it.

The big raccoon *skrarg-skrarg-skrarg*ed, and Ashwin raised the pinecone, ready to fire. All of its buddies were gone, and we had enough pinecones to drive it away all night. But the big raccoon still paced back and forth, refusing to give up. I kinda wanted to snatch the pinecone from Ashwin and chuck it, but Nuts squeaked, "Let it fly, Canela," and Buggies crossed his arms and gave a little nod. Since Buggies was the OIC, it was his call.

Ashwin chucked the pinecone.

I didn't think he would get a hit. Not this far away.

But he did.

The big raccoon yelped, retreated across the empty basketball courts after the other raccoons, and vanished into the dark. It was awesome watching that raccoon run away.

We all sat side by side with our feet hanging down the wide metal slide under the tall wooden tower.

"We won!" squeaked Nuts.

"Say it, don't spray it," I told him.

Mila cackled, and Ashwin pushed her down the slide. We all climbed on top of the monkey bars in the dark. Up there, we could see the golf course, the whole school, snatches of downtown, the fenced-in freeway overpass, and the dark mesa. We could do whatever we wanted and nobody would bug us.

No parents.

No teachers.

No raccoons.

And no Danny Vega.

20.
The Spoils of War

Me and Ashwin kept a lookout for a while in our goofy armor, but we knew those raccoons weren't coming back. It was cool being up on the monkey bars with nobody else around, and we didn't want to leave. We played on the whole playground, climbed the towers, took turns on the swings, and rode the slides. Nuts and Buggies went down the big slide like a hundred times. Forwards. Backwards. On their feet. On their hands. Spinning down on their fuzzy backs. Somewhere in the middle of that night, we all heard a train, and Nuts and Buggies came to attention, saluting each other.

"You are relieved of your command," squeaked Nuts.

"Yes sir, Sergeant Nuts," Buggies said.

And just like that, Nuts was the OIC. Guess they really did take turns.

Ashwin gave me this look—I think you probably know what it said—and Mila, she gave me one too. "I guess we could try it," I said, scrunching my mouth.

"Ashwin's the highest rank, and he's older so . . ."

Ashwin grinned. "Nah-ah, man. It's got to be Polka Dots. She won the war for us."

Mila hopped up off the trike, coming to attention.

"Caballero, Canela, you are relieved of your command," she said.

"Yes sir, Polka Dots." Me and Ashwin both saluted, and then we taught her our oath.

It felt kinda silly, but it also felt right. I decided I liked having Mila as a fellow knight, and even though I didn't think I would, I liked giving her the trike for keeps. But most of all, I liked knowing that I kept my promise to Mom about keeping Mila safe.

After the skunks switched ranks, they went right back to riding the slides. When they got tired of that, the skunks and Mila took turns riding the trike around the playground. They were pretending to guard it but mostly showing off their tricks. Mila even tried riding in the bucket while the skunks pedaled, but she was too heavy for them.

"Hop off," she said. "My turn! Want to ride in the bucket?"

"Negative, kiddo. Time for us to get back to base," Buggies said.

"Time for eats and sleeps!" Nuts squeaked.

"We'll ride back with you," I said. "You know, just to make sure you get there okay."

Ashwin snatched up his bike. I dragged Steed out from

under the playground. It was a little dusty and scratched in a couple spots, but that only made me love it more. It had been through battle with me, and we'd won.

We all rode off in a tight triangle formation again— Mila leading the way, me and Ashwin coming behind, watching each flank for red-eyed raccoons. Our armor crackled a little, but our formation stayed pretty quiet. Mila stopped on the path next to her pink butterfly net, and Nuts snatched it up. The skunks unscrewed the extendable handle, folded it in half, and stuffed it into the bucket between them.

I made everybody use the crosswalk at Las Positas again. This time, Mila did get off to walk, while the skunks rode the trike solo. Mila even held my hand. Then, coasting down the hill, everybody went silent. When we got to Mr. Mendoza's back path, Ashwin leaned over to scoop up our perfume-filled water guns. He tossed them into the basket in front of his handle-bars, and they made a big *clang*. Both skunks turned to glare at him. Then Nuts squeaked, "Forward roll, Polka Dots. The battlefield is clear."

When Mila pedaled down the sidewalk, the taken-apart net *tink-tink-tink*ed in the trike bucket. I thought about the noise that had been coming from Mila's backpack on the walk to school.

"Hey, Polka Dots," I whispered. "Did you have that thing in your backpack all day?"

"Of course! I told you I had a plan."

"Quiet, Polka Dots! We're going in silent," squeaked Nuts.

Mila was so serious. I couldn't help laughing just a little. Our armor had been great, but our weapons turned out to be duds. She had totally saved our butts with the net. Having Mila for a little sister was like having a secret weapon. A weapon so totally secret even *I* didn't know I had it.

When we passed by Danny Vega's house, I couldn't help thinking about Johnny again. More than all the trash-talking, and launching missiles, that's what bugged me the most. That Johnny was friends with a dude like Danny, but not with us. I guess I still kind of hoped that Johnny would change his mind—that all that stuff my dad said didn't matter. But I knew it did, even if I didn't really get why. Maybe the skunks were right. Maybe some things don't have any explanation, no matter how much you want them to.

Maybe I could have gotten the skunks to sneak into Danny's garage and spray his bike seat for us. See how many friends he'd have after that. I laughed under my breath, thinking about Danny's butt smelling like skunk spray *for the rest of his life*.

But I didn't ask.

I decided that wasn't an honorable thing to do.

The war with the raccoons, I could understand that easy. They were just *messed up*, and no way were the skunks ever going to be able to work it out with them and take turns on the playground. I mean, the raccoons couldn't even talk. But I knew stinking up Danny's bike seat wasn't gonna fix anything. I was pretty sure nothing I did was gonna make Johnny my friend again, but I knew way too much about Johnny to think of him as some bad guy, like from a book or a movie. And Ashwin didn't even seem to notice Danny's house when we rode past. If he could let it go, I decided I should too.

At Stink Base, the skunks tumbled out of the bucket on the back of Mila's trike, and Nuts heaved the door open. The pulleys creaked softly.

"This reminds me, Caballero," said Nuts. "Know where we might find a two-inch PVC pipe, a battery powered drill, and an old vacuum?"

"What are you guys gonna do with all that?" Ashwin asked.

"That's top-secret intelligence," Buggies said.

"Not even chocolate-covered slugs could make us talk," Nuts added.

Well, Mila rode her trike around them in a slow circle, giving them her I'm-never-giving-up-so-just-tell-me-already stare. "Ahhhh, come on!" she said. "We helped you win the war!"

Ashwin leaned down over the stupid flower basket of his sister's old bike.

"Yeah, we're allies now. You can tell us," I said.

Nuts and Buggies gave each other a long look, and Nuts shrugged.

"We're still early in the development process," said Buggies. "But we've got an idea for some new artillery."

"I call it the Cannon of Stink," squeaked Nuts, bugging out his little black eyes.

Me and Ashwin grinned at each other. "We have a book you guys have *got* to see," I told them.

21.
The Pancakes

When the sky started to get pink and peek through the branches above Stink Base, Nuts and Buggies unplugged their twinkle lights and dove into their bunks. The Midnight War was over. For now, anyway.

"Good night, Sir Buggies. Good night, Sir Nuts," I said saluting.

"Make sure you're not sighted by the enemy on the way out," said Buggies.

"And leave the three-wheeled creaker where we can get it tomorrow night, Polka Dots," called Nuts.

"I will," Mila said, pulling their little dishrag curtains closed. "They're so cute," she said on the way up the ramp.

"I don't know if *cute* is the right word, kid," Ashwin said.

The skunks were snoring before we even closed the hedge door, but we were all still too excited to sleep. We decided to go home for Mom's Saturday morning chocolate-chip pancakes. Me and Ashwin swished back and forth on our bikes, but kinda slow, so Mila could lead the way. The sky was getting brighter every second, and the fog was creeping up over our city, coming up from the beach until it hung at the edge of the freeway. Right then, I heard the train coming. Going south, I think. I can tell the difference. Swear. We stopped at the edge of Mr. Mendoza's driveway. Mila bumped into my back wheel, and I heard a little *tink-clunk.*

"Hey, what's going on? I thought we were getting pancakes!" she grumbled.

"Shhhh." I pointed to Mr. Mendoza's house. His porch light was on and the curtains were open.

"Do you think he's waiting for us?" Ashwin asked.

I listened hard for a minute. "Nah—I bet he just fell asleep in front of the TV again. But let's get past his driveway quick, okay?"

Ashwin saluted me. "Yes sir, Caballero."

"Cut it out. Let's go." I nodded to Mila.

She nodded back and went first, pedaling as fast as she could. Me and Ashwin zoomed after. When we got to our driveway, we threw the stinky black garbage bags away, and Mila scrambled around the house, putting the goggles and boots and stuff back.

"Do you think we should tell Dad the skunks are going to borrow his drill?" Mila asked.

"No!" me and Ashwin said at the same time.

We ended up in a heap on the fuzzy brown couch

watching a cartoon. Something with a talking penguin. That cartoon seemed really funny after the night we'd had. Me and Ashwin kept cracking up.

"You guys are up early," Mom said, padding down the hall in her sweats and sock-monkey slippers. She walked straight into the kitchen without even glancing our way.

"We got my trike back from the skunks," shouted Mila.

Me and Ashwin both shushed her.

"Oh, yeah?" Mom said, taking her mixing bowls out of the cupboard. She looked at us sitting there on the couch in our stinky sweats. Right at me.

"Yeah, Mateo helped," Mila said, elbowing me in the side.

"Your Dad thought he might," Mom said and smiled that smile. The special Saturday-morning smile. Morning Mom was better than after-work Mom, but Saturday-morning Mom was the best. She never asked too many questions. She wore her sweats until noon. She made pancakes with chocolate chips, and she smiled that smile.

The doorbell rang. "Who could that be?" Mom said, wiping flour off her hands. "Mateo, can you go answer the door?"

When I opened the door, my mouth fell open.

Mr. Mendoza.

He was holding Mila's extendable butterfly net. It had one of her pink sticky nametags on it. When he saw me standing there in my stinky red sweats, he knew I'd been the kid in his garden in the middle of the night. I could tell. His eyes bulged behind his thick square glasses, and he leaned in so close I could smell his breath. And man, it was gross.

"I knew it was you—you little thug! I knew you were up to something, and now I have proof!" he said, waving Mila's net in my face. "First those skunks, always trotting through my orchard, then tricycle tracks, then boys on bikes."

"Wait a second. You knew about the skunks?" I asked.

Mr. Mendoza sputtered, and I wrinkled my nose at his breath. He shoved the butterfly net into my hands and pushed his glasses up onto his nose. "Keep those creatures off my path and out of my hydrangea bushes," he said, poking me in the chest with his wrinkled finger.

"Uh . . . okay, Mr. Mendoza," I said.

He stomped down the front steps. I watched with my mouth still open as his stooped back disappeared down the sidewalk.

"Who was it?" Mom asked from the kitchen.

"Ah, it was Mr. Mendoza," I said. "He brought back Mila's butterfly net."

"That was nice of him," said Mom.

"Yeah . . . it was," I said, staring at the net. It must have bumped out of the trike bucket on the way home.

"Why didn't he tell?" Ashwin whispered when I got back to the couch.

"I guess maybe he thinks he's going crazy or something. Like, what would happen if he told everyone two talking skunks were riding a trike through his backyard every night?"

"Awesome! Mr. Mendoza can never get us in trouble again!" Ashwin said.

Dad woke up and made coffee. I saw Mom whisper in his ear. I pretended to just be watching cartoons, but really I was watching them, 'cause keeping an eye on things is still one of my jobs, even when Mila's the OIC.

"Lemme hear it, Mama. Come on," Dad said, laughing.

"You were right," said Mom.

Then Dad squeezed her, which he almost never does when she's wearing the red Stanford sweatshirt. I guess maybe he doesn't really hate it. He whispered something in her ear, something in Spanish. Mom's coffee spilled a little, right on the sweatshirt, and she pushed Dad away, but not before she let him kiss her. That's when I stopped watching them. I leaned back against the fuzzy couch and finished that cartoon.

There are still things I can't figure out about my neighborhood. All that stuff with Johnny and Danny and Martin and Spanish. I don't really get that yet. But until I figure it out, I'm just gonna go with my gut and keep trying to be a good knight.

Plus, there are some things I *do* understand. I

understand chocolate-chip pancakes on Saturday morning. I understand Mila is like a secret weapon. And I understand my best friend, Ashwin, has pretty good aim, even if he is a little weird.

That's enough. For now.

When we were done, Dad pushed his plate back and poured another cup of coffee. Mom dipped her finger in the bowl of whipped cream.

"Let's go race my new trike." Mila took a last sip of milk and made the same noise Dad does after his first sip of coffee.

"New trike? What new trike?" Mom said, all worried again.

"I told you. Mateo got the trike back. He *gave* it to me. For keeps." Mila shuffled off toward the door. "Bet you I can make it down the driveway faster than you," she yelled.

I followed her out there. "Mila, it's not going to be faster now just because it's yours."

"Oh, man," Ashwin said, thumping down the front steps.

I swung a leg over Steed. Mila plunked herself down on her trike and grabbed the handles hard.

"Ready, set, go!" Ashwin shouted.

We raced down the driveway, and it was close.

But Mila won.

Ashwin asked me if I let her.

"Nah," I said. "I guess I'm pretty tired from all that riding last night."

"Really?" Mila asked, staring at me crooked.

"That's the truth," I said.

And it sort of was.

DISPATCHES FROM THE
MIDNIGHT WAR COMMAND LOG

[Declassified in accordance with a request on February 10, 2016 by Sgt. Caballero on the authority of OIC Sgt. Buggies]

While declassified, the included materials may not be duplicated or distributed through unofficial channels.

~~(TOP SECRET)~~

Midnight Command Log: January 28
Officer in Charge: Sergeant Buggies

Notes: Our mission to acquire a new transport
device was completed without incident
or injury. Sergeant Nuts is intent upon
returning to the test site on Caballero
Road in order to assess possible future
acquisitions. I remain doubtful as to the
maneuverability of any large vehicles on
site, but that driveway has particularly
excellent eats, so we will be returning.
Sergeant Nuts also suggests a series of
midnight training missions on the new
vehicle before the equipment is taken into
battle, and I concur.

This document contains information concerning
the defense of the neighborhood playground.
Its transmission or the revelation of its
contents in any way to an unauthorized person
is prohibited by Skunk Code 1978:STNK.

Midday Command Log: January 28

Officer in Charge: Sergeant Nuts

Notes: Perimeter alarm triggered at approximately 1700 hours. Checked for intruders and found no sign of forced entry. Stink Base perimeter is secure. Probably just kids. Back to my bunk after a quick inventory!

Current Acquisitions List:

~~6 tarpaulins (Stink Base)~~
assorted pulleys (Stink Base)
chocolate-covered almonds (General Acquisitions)

(~~TOP SECRET~~)

Midnight Command Log: January 29

Officer in Charge: Sergeant Buggies

Notes: While securing evening rations (which were excellent per usual) and assessing an equipment acquisition at our favored test site, mission security was compromised. The male juvenile resident [code name Caballero] ambushed our party from behind the trash receptacles. Sergeant Nuts deployed one shot of stink, but Caballero continued to give chase. We were able to mount our new vehicle and evade further discovery. The planned training mission continued without further complication aside from a brief sighting by the elderly male resident [code name Geezer]. Our Midnight War offensive will commence at 2300 hours as planned.

This document contains information concerning the defense of the neighborhood playground. Its transmission or the revelation of its contents in any way to an unauthorized person is prohibited by Skunk Code 1978:STNK.

Midday Command Log: January 29

Officer in Charge: Sergeant Nuts

Notes: The perimeter alarm was triggered TWICE between 1700 and 1800 hours. This time I sighted the juveniles [code names Caballero, Canela, and Polka Dots]. Polka Dots was utilizing a pushable four-wheeled vehicle with impressive cargo capacity. The vehicle's transport space far exceeds that of the trike bucket. When Sergeant Buggies wakes up, I'm going to suggest we put the push thingy on the acquisitions list.

Current Acquisitions List:
Polka-dotted push thingy (General Acquisitions)

This document contains information concerning the defense of the neighborhood playground. Its transmission or the revelation of its contents in any way to an unauthorized person is prohibited by Skunk Code 1978:STNK.

Midnight Command Log: January 30

Officer in Charge: Sergeant Buggies

Notes: Formed an alliance with Caballero, Canela, and Polka Dots in the Midnight War. All parties distinguished themselves with great honor on the battlefield, showing courage and loyalty. Victory was secured! Sergeant Nuts and I performed the requisite wiggle dance atop the play structure. Those slides are something else!

This document contains information concerning the defense of the neighborhood playground. Its transmission or the revelation of its contents in any way to an unauthorized person is prohibited by Skunk Code 1978:STNK.

Midday Command Log: January 30

Officer in Charge: Sergeant Nuts

Notes: Our new allies, Sgts. Caballero, Canela & Polka Dots, promise to be a rich source of Military Appropriations (so long as we agree to implement new oversight protocols in our current acquisitions program). Project code name Cannon of Stink is ready for stage-two implementation.

Acquisitions list:
~~electric drill (TCOS)~~
2 inch PVC piping (TCOS)
leaf blower or old vacuum (TCOS)
chocolate-covered grasshoppers (General Acquisitions)

Acknowledgments

A book is the creation of many hands, so my first thank you is for everyone at Lerner Books who helped make my story into a real thing that I can hold in mine. Thank you to Teagan White for pink raccoons. For a cover as lovely and weird and funny as I could have wished for. Thank you to my editor, Greg Hunter, who I'm pretty sure knew what this book was about before I did and who helped me find the best way to tell my story.

Thank you to Erica Rand Silverman, who has lifted me up with her patient enthusiasm—a thing it seems almost impossible to have, but she has it. Plus, she likes all my dumb jokes and has never once called me too quirky.

Thank you to my writing friends, almost all gleaned from the Society of Children's Book Writers and Illustrators, for reading and questioning and then reading again all along the way. A special thank you to John Parra for reading and saying nice things at just the right time. Just when I needed it.

To my sisters, who are like secret weapons, ones you have all the time, whether you want them or not, who know that I'm not very good at saying thank you—I'll just say, I'm glad I have you (most of the time) and I hope you don't mind if I continue to put all your cuteness and weirdness and drama into my books. Because that's my plan.

Last, for just living in Santa Barbara, I feel a great debt. Like any city, it is filled with small communities, pockets of people, and streets and parks. But this city between the mountains and the strangely south-facing coast, with its fog and festivals, is the only one I call mine, and I'm so happy to share it with you.

About the Author

Robin Yardi lives in the California foothills, where—every once in a while, in the dark of night—a skunk or two will sneak by. She loves good stories, animals of all sorts, homemade cakes, and kids. She thinks kids are way cooler than grownups, which is why she writes just for them. Visit her online at www.robinyardi.com.